THE OFFICIAL
ONE PIECE
COLORING BOOK

SCHOLASTIC INC.

All rights reserved. Published by Scholastic Inc., *Publishers since 1920.*
SCHOLASTIC and associated logos are trademarks and/or registered
trademarks of Scholastic Inc.

ISBN 978-1-339-01747-1

10 9 8 7 6 5 4 3 2   23 24 25 26 27

Printed in the U.S.A.   40

First printing 2023

Book design by Salena Mahina & Elliane Mellet

Background icons throughout © Shutterstock.com

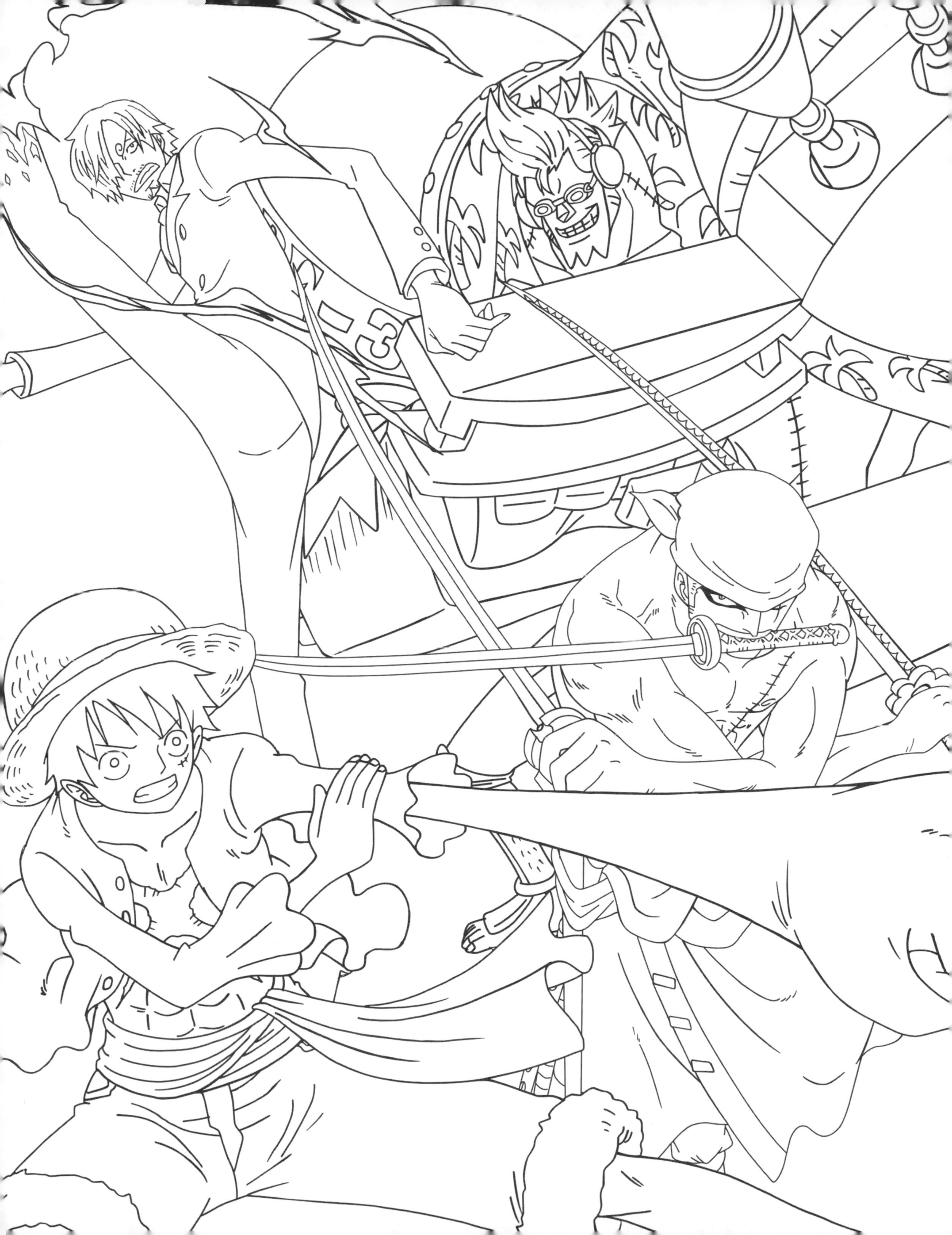

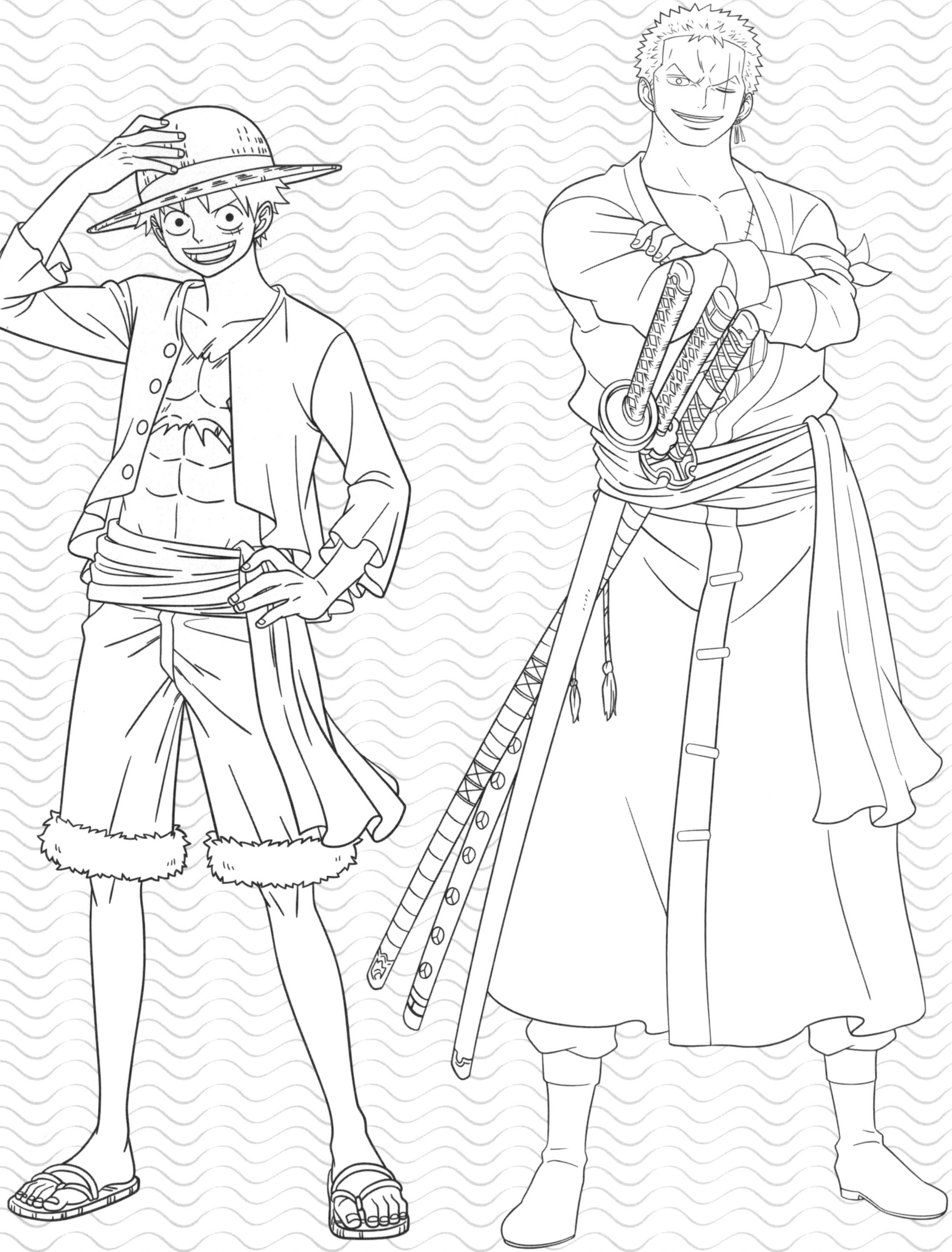

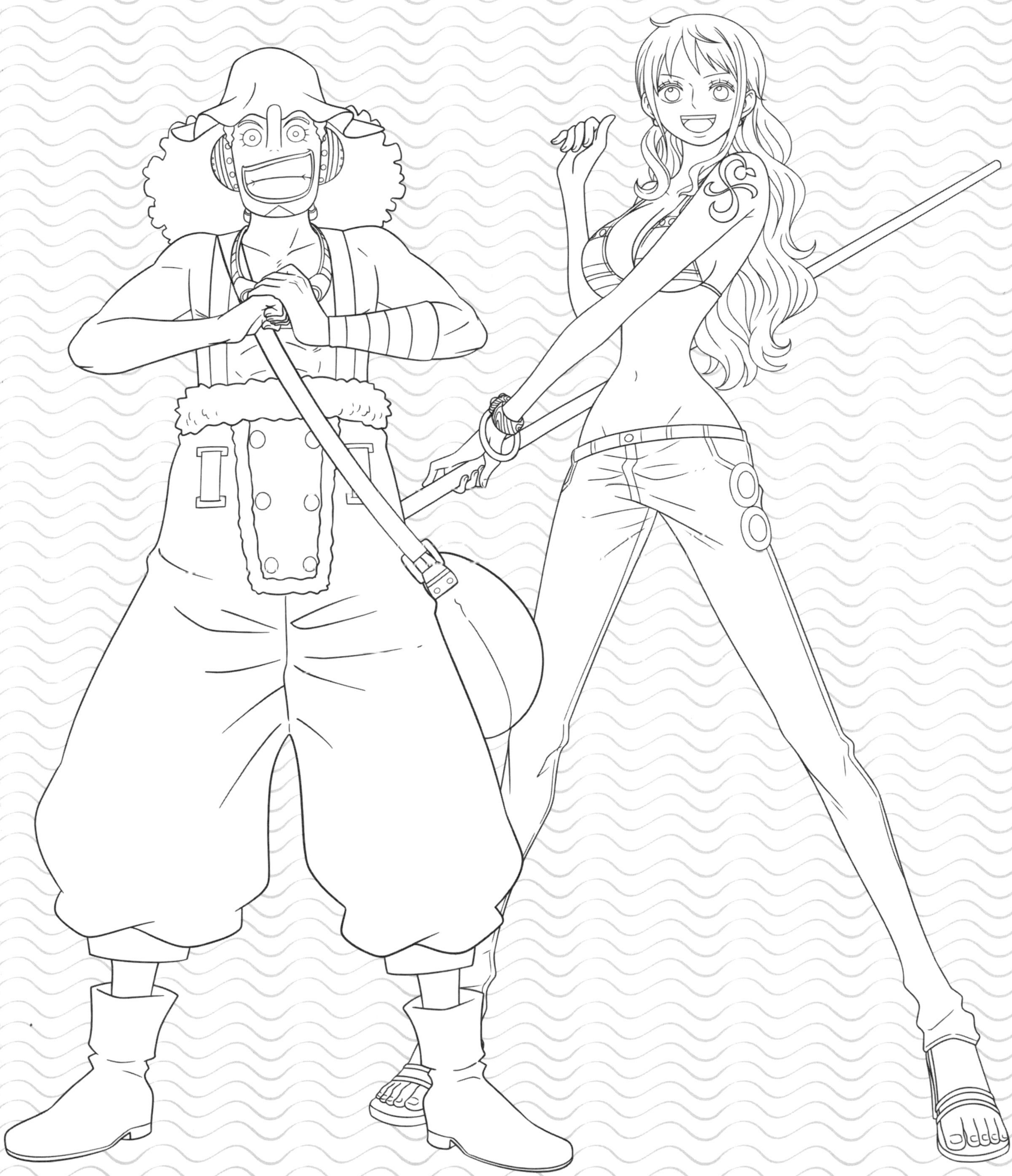

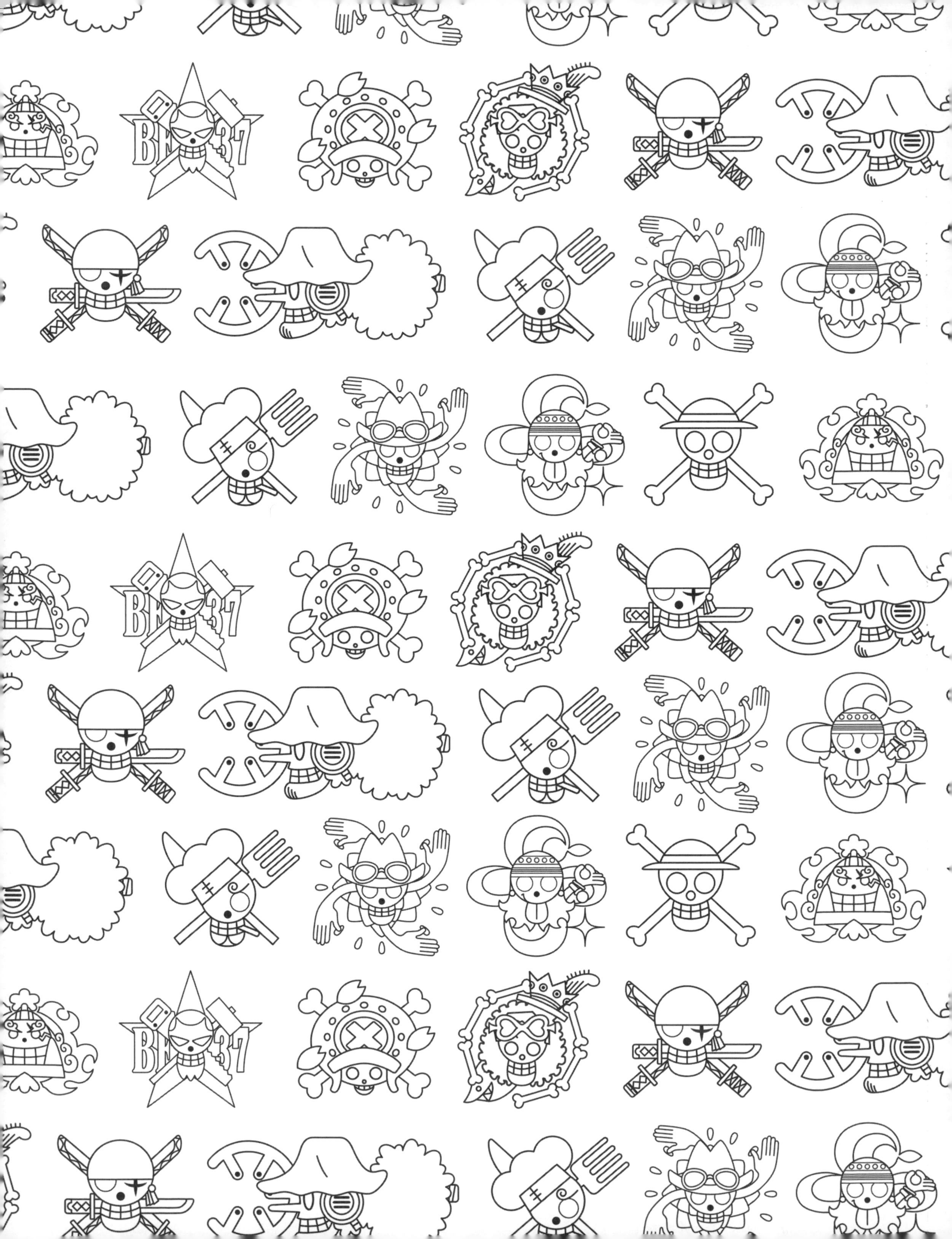

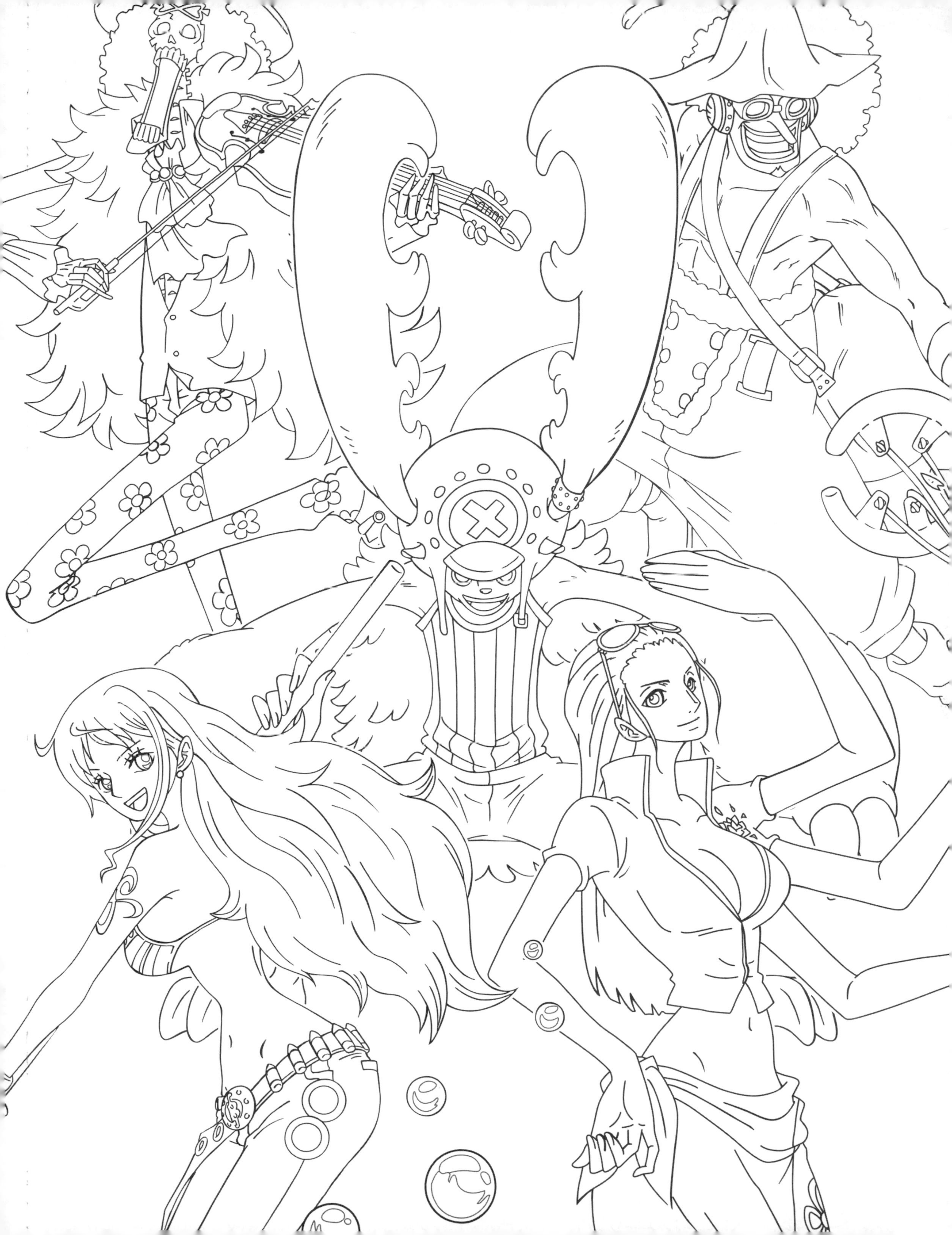

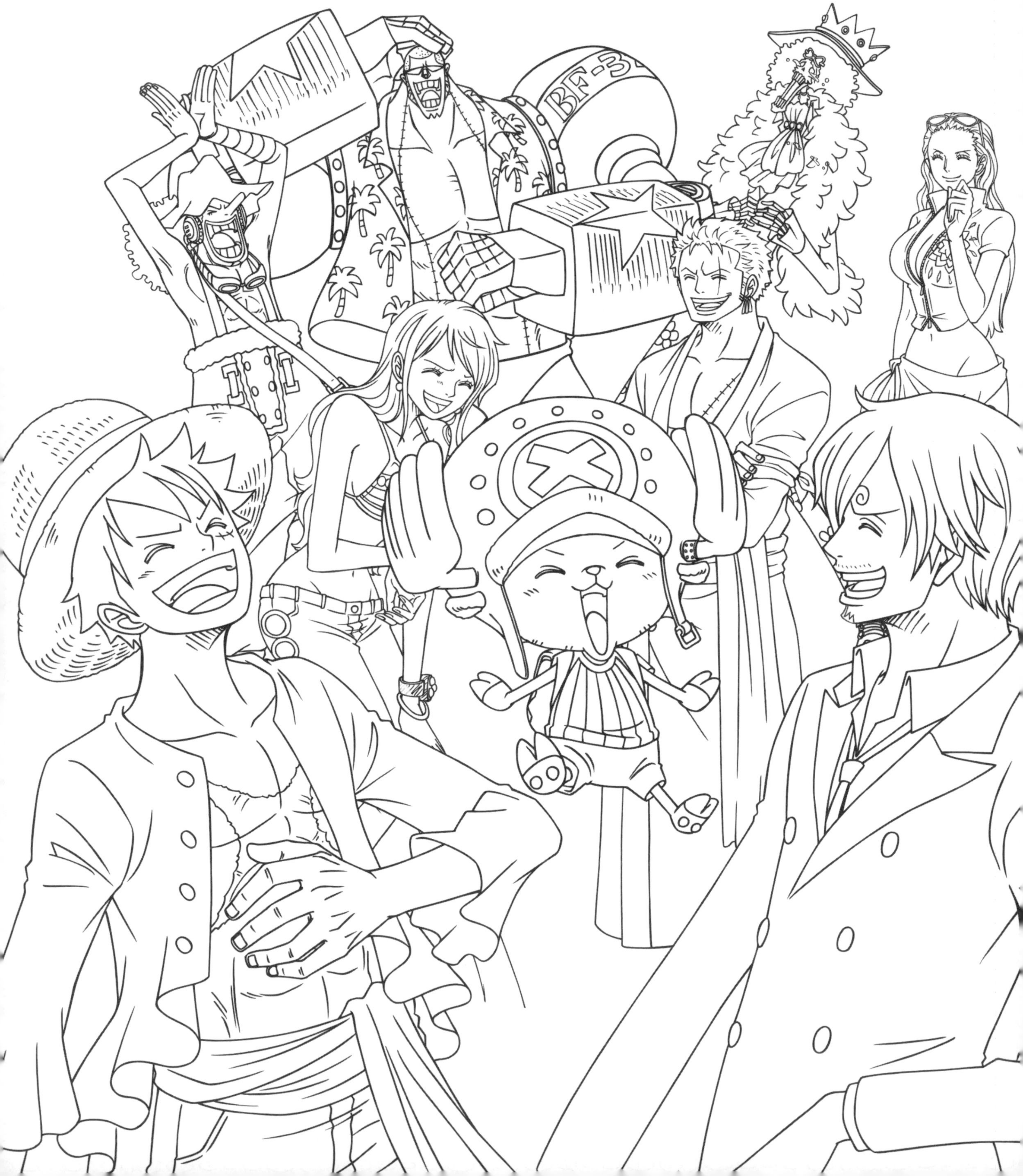
BF-3

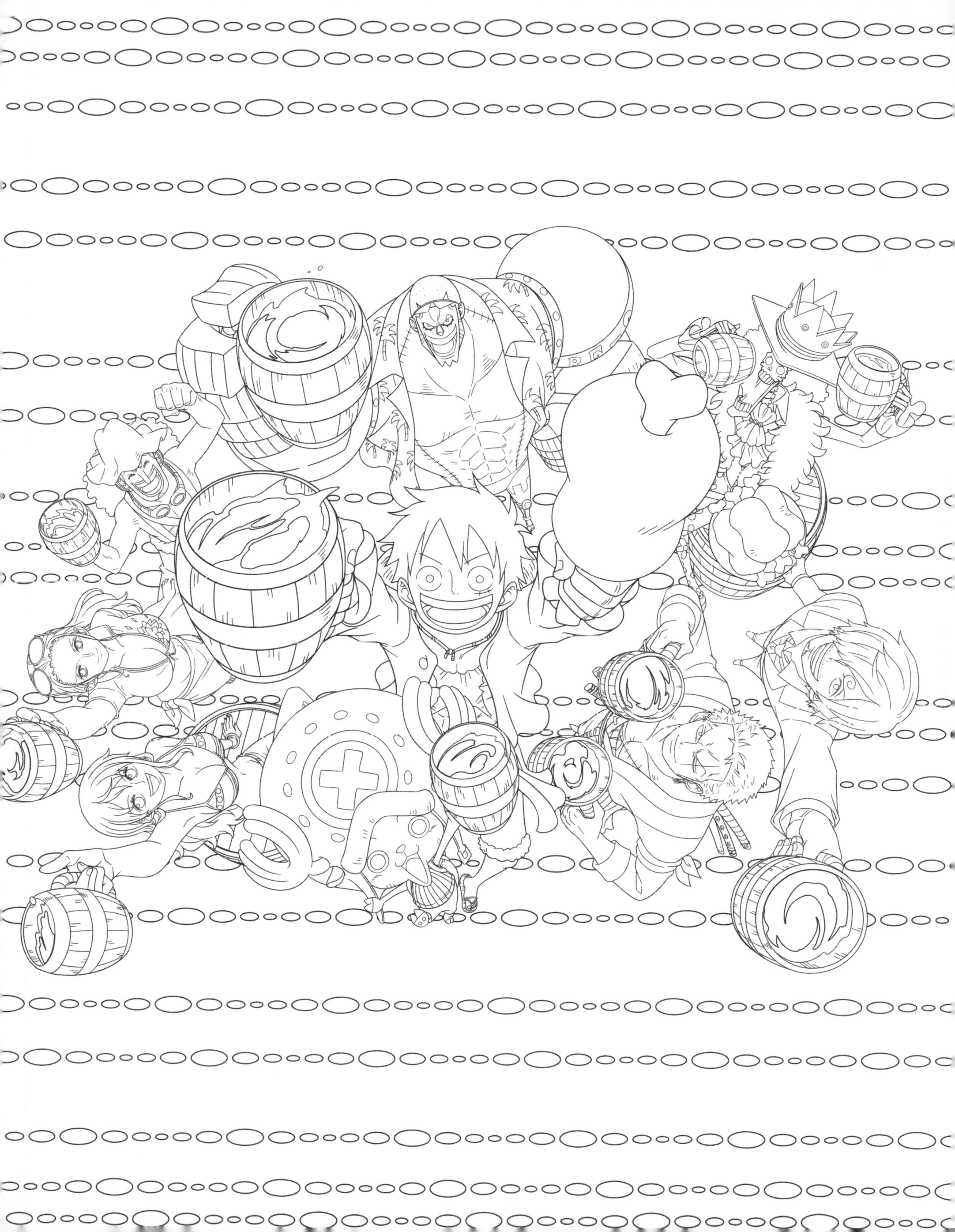

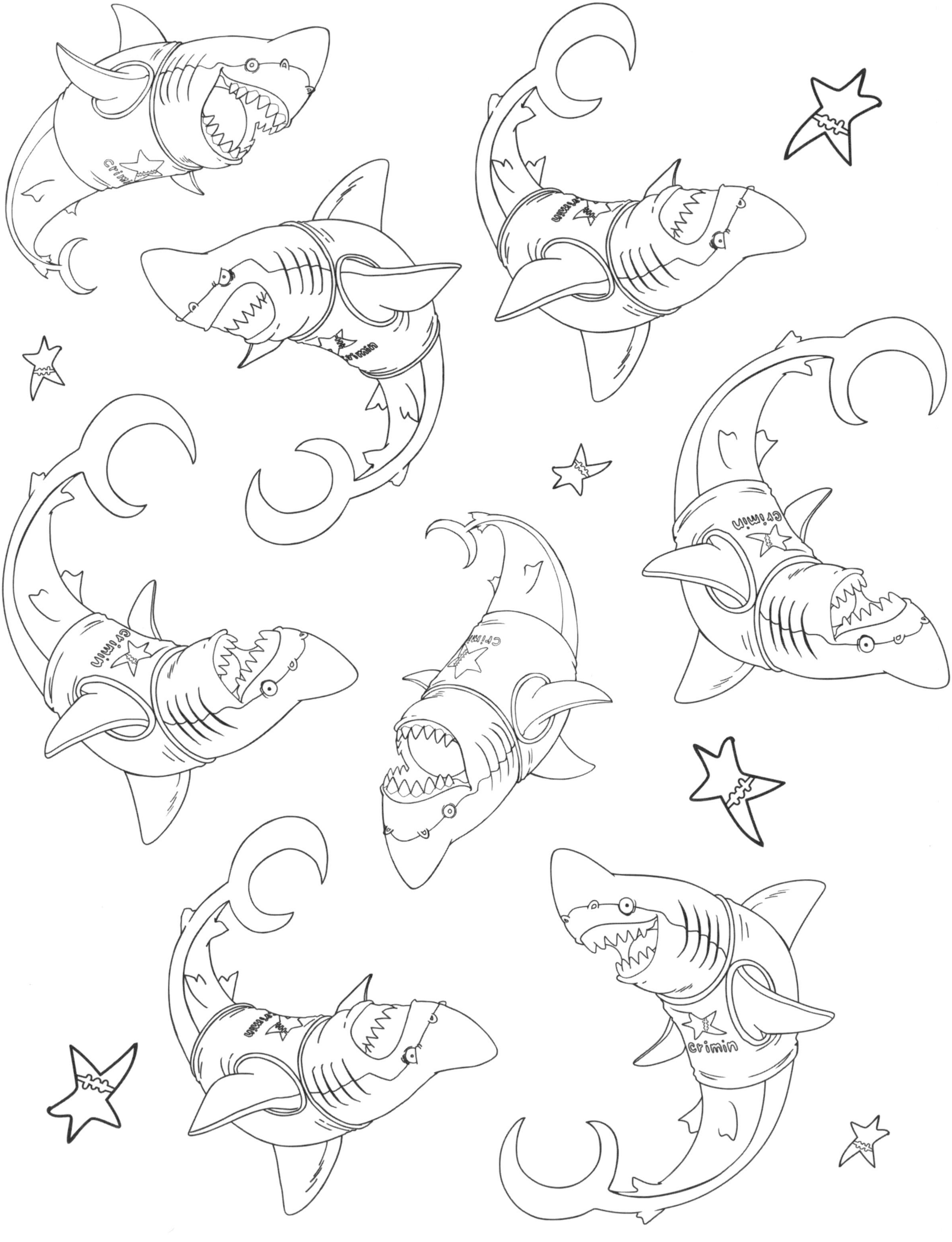
crimin

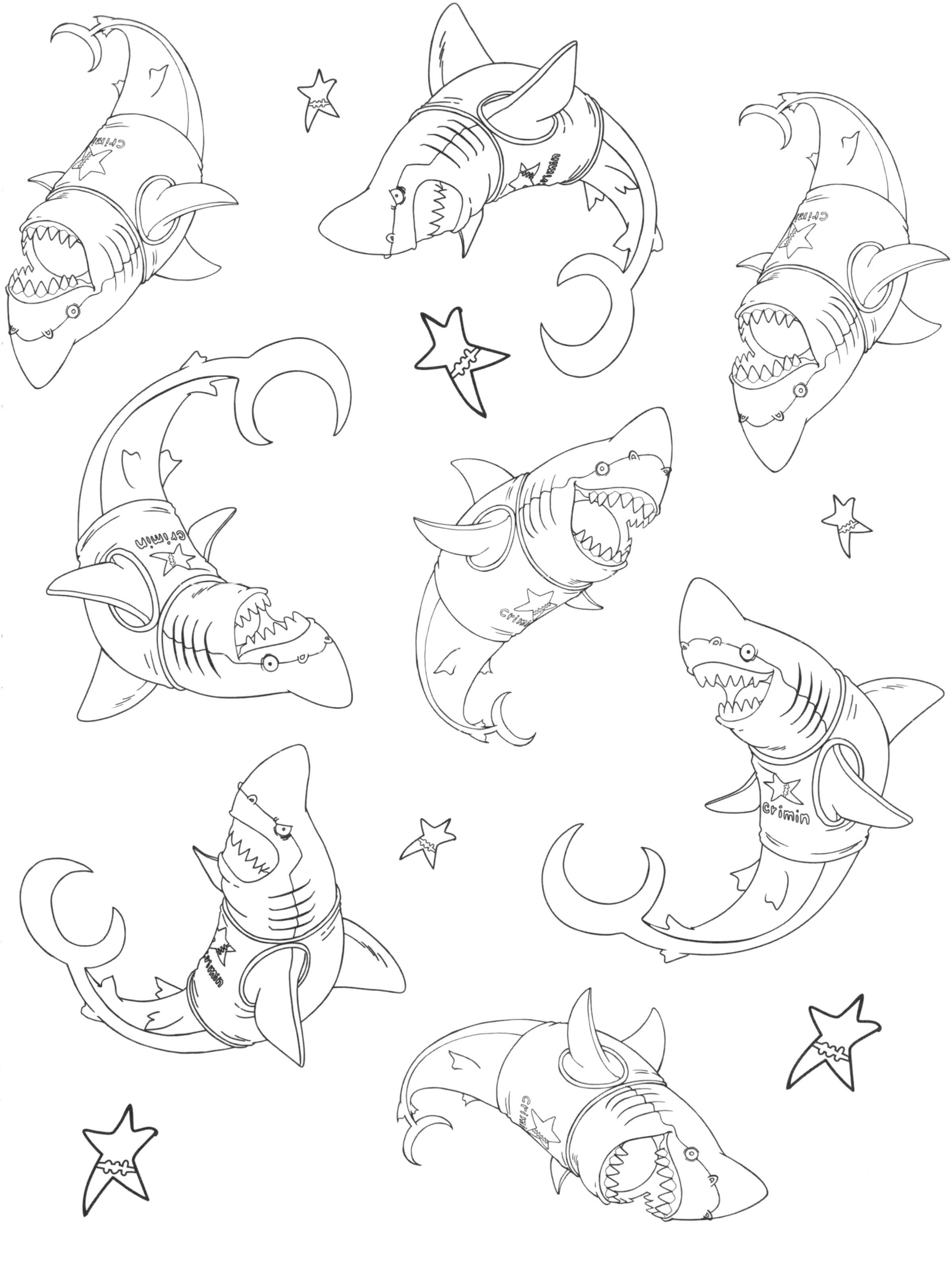
crimin
crimin

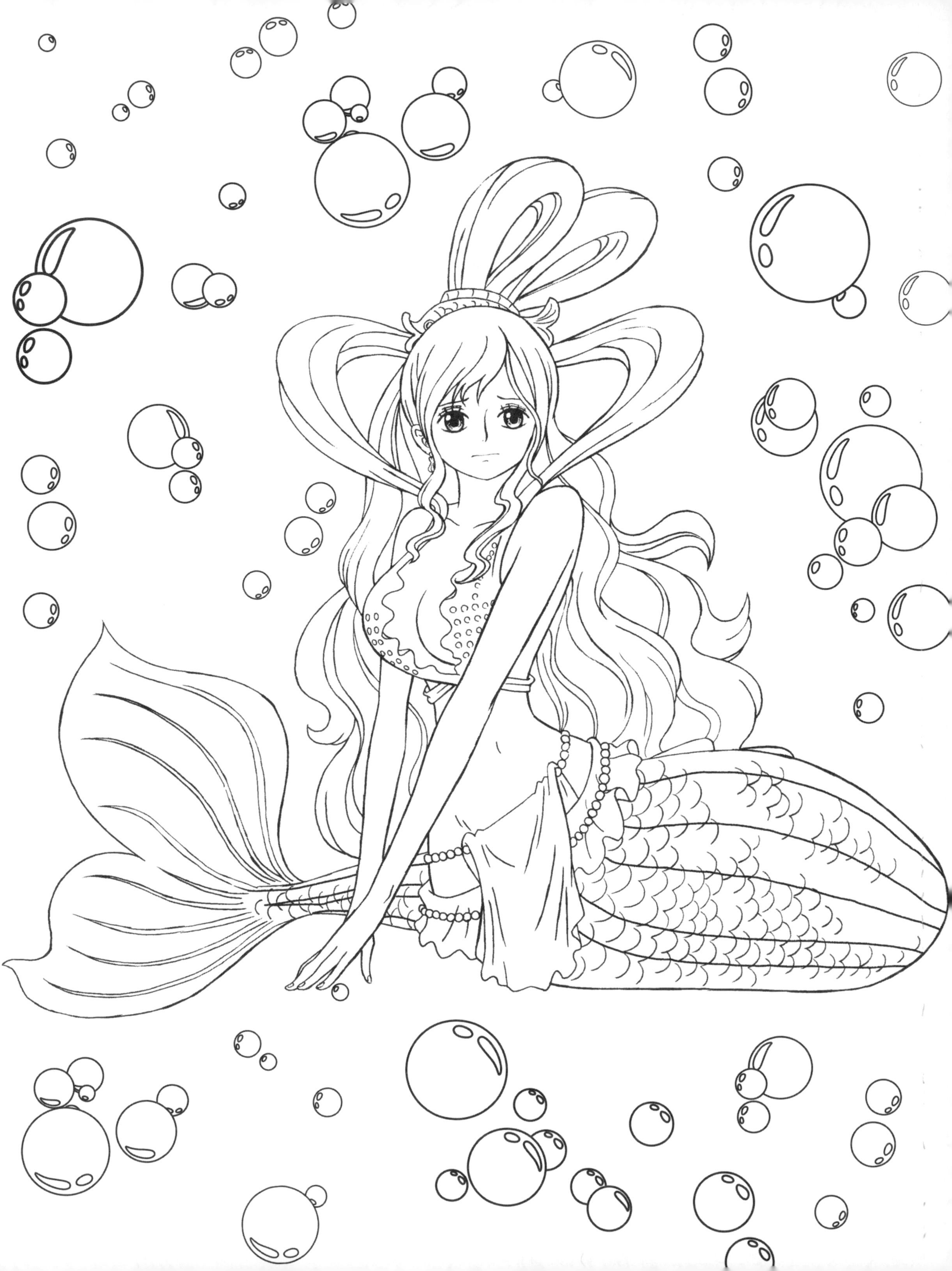

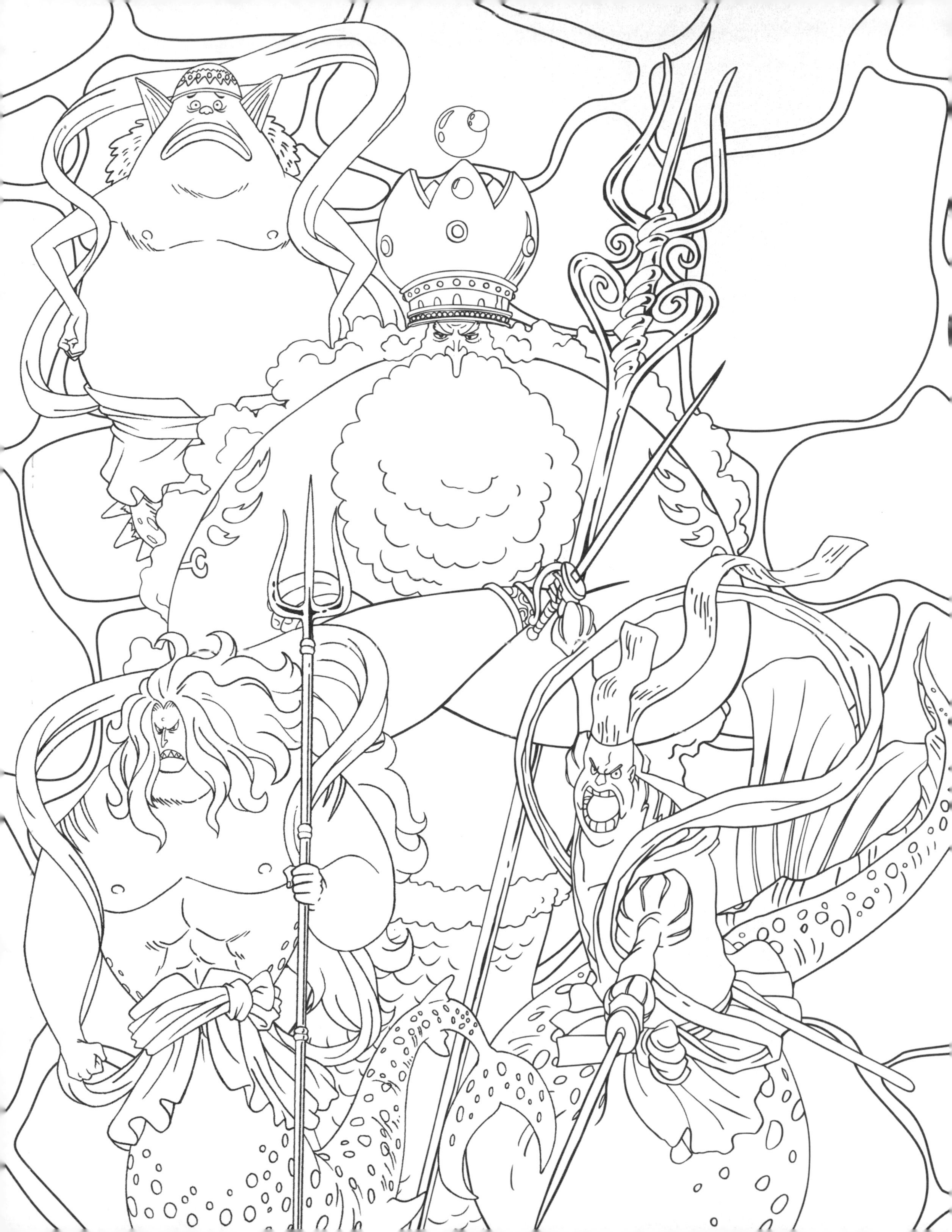

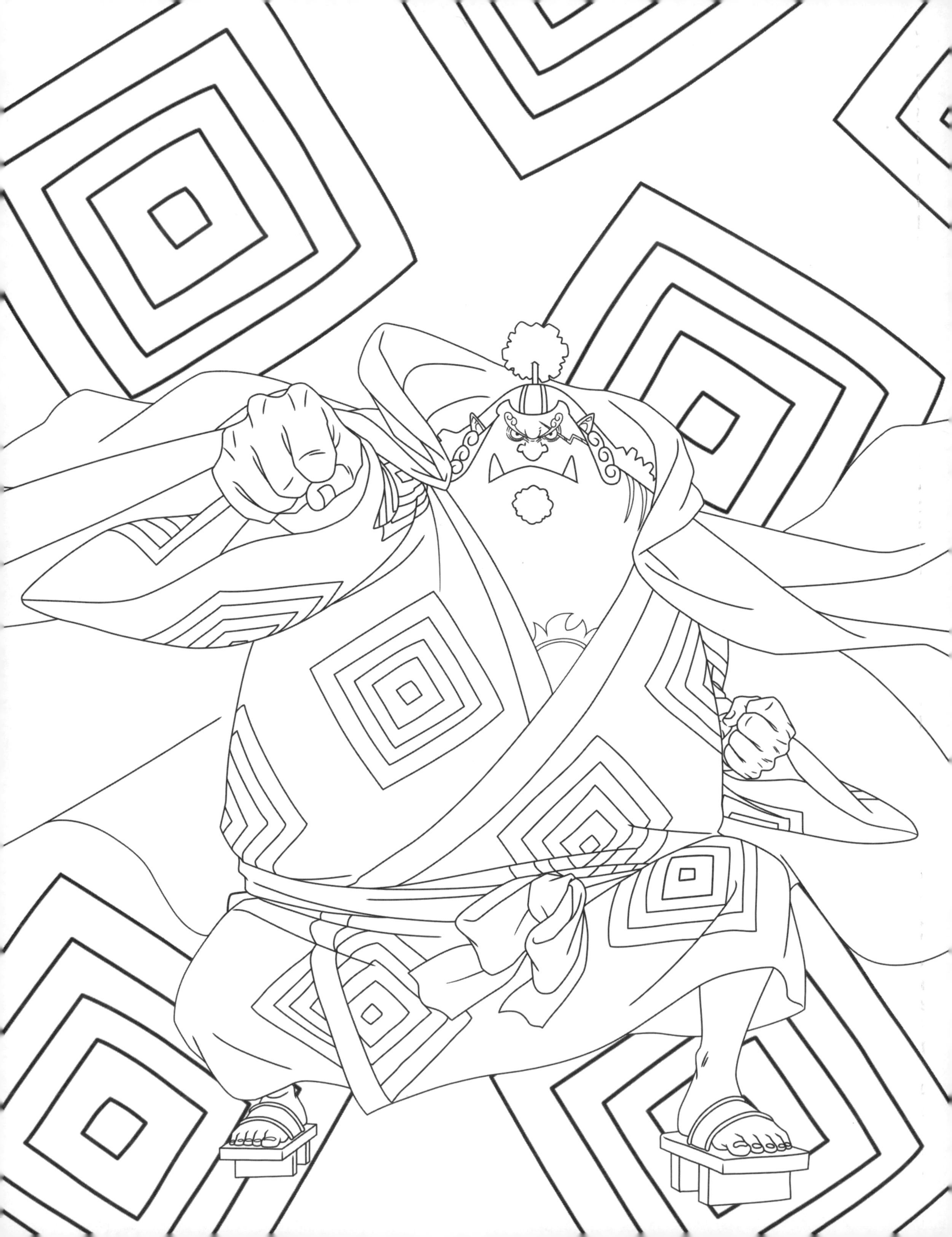

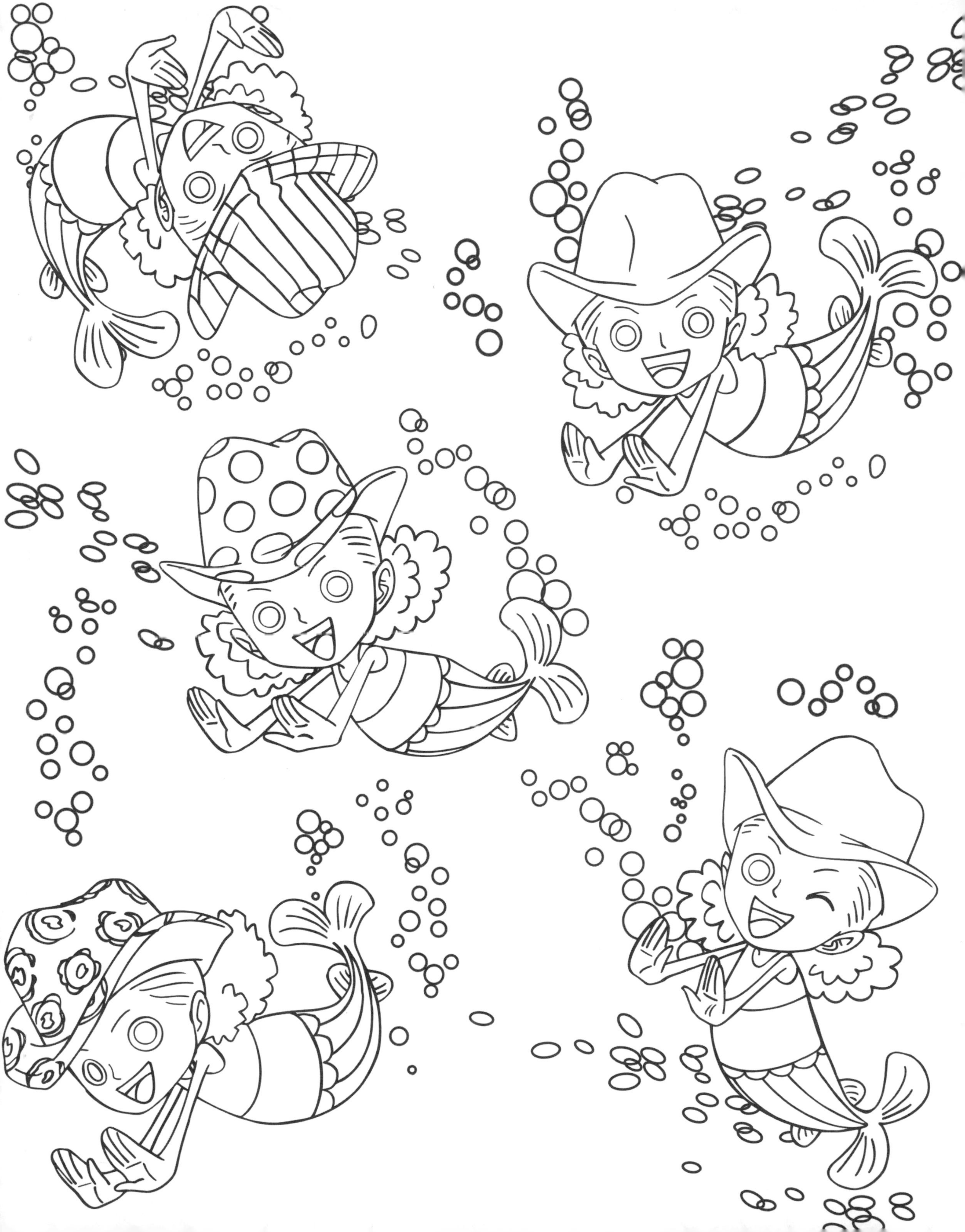

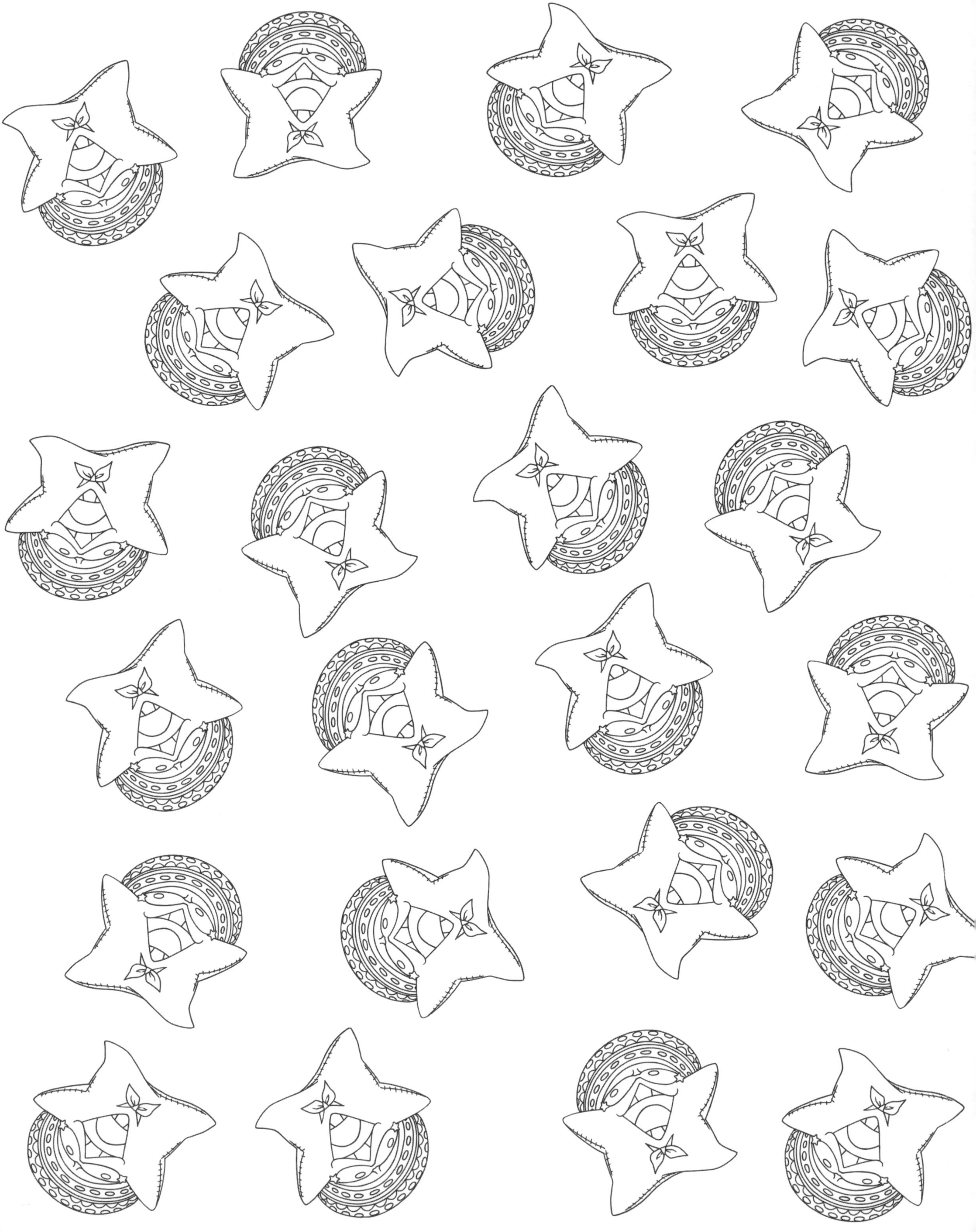

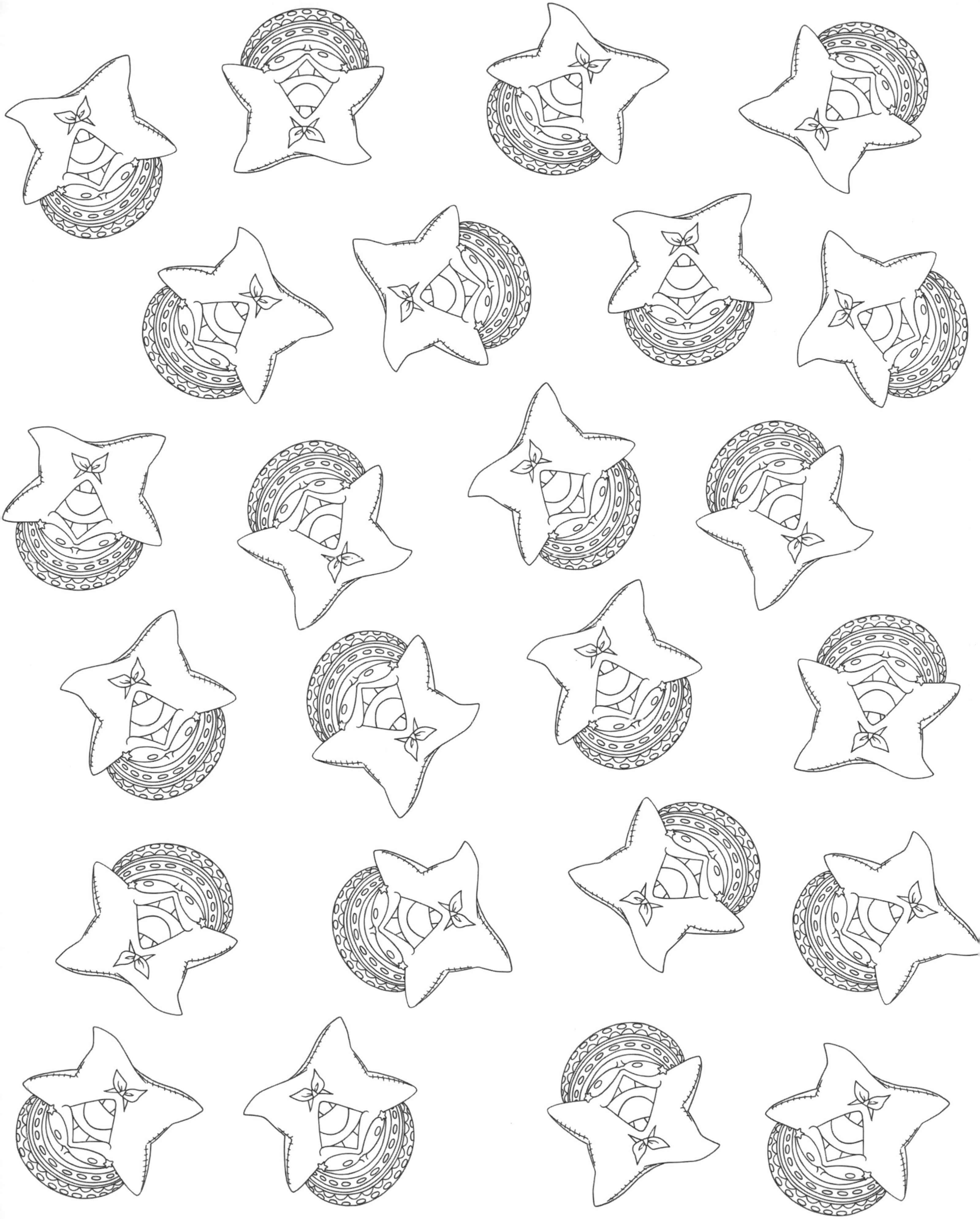

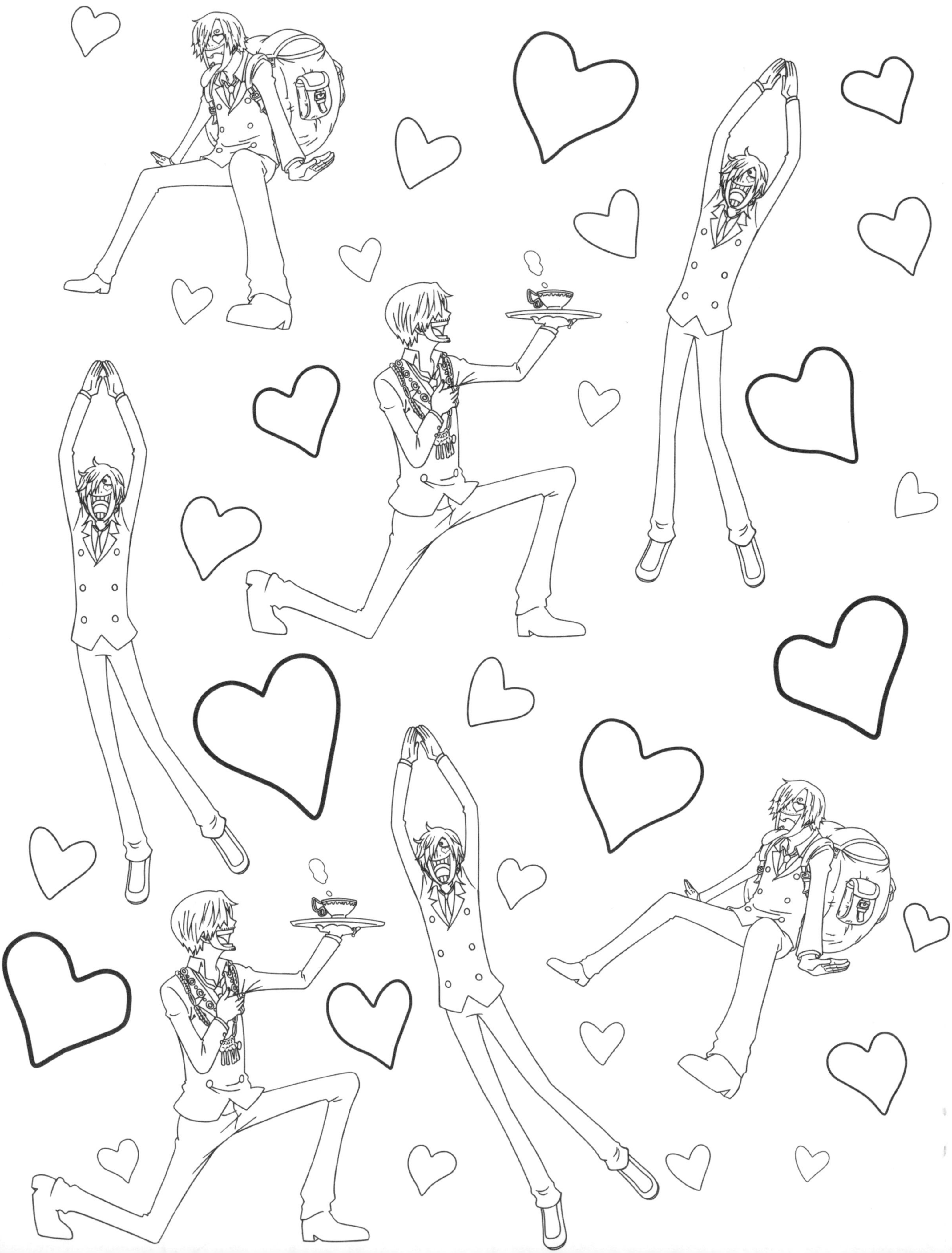

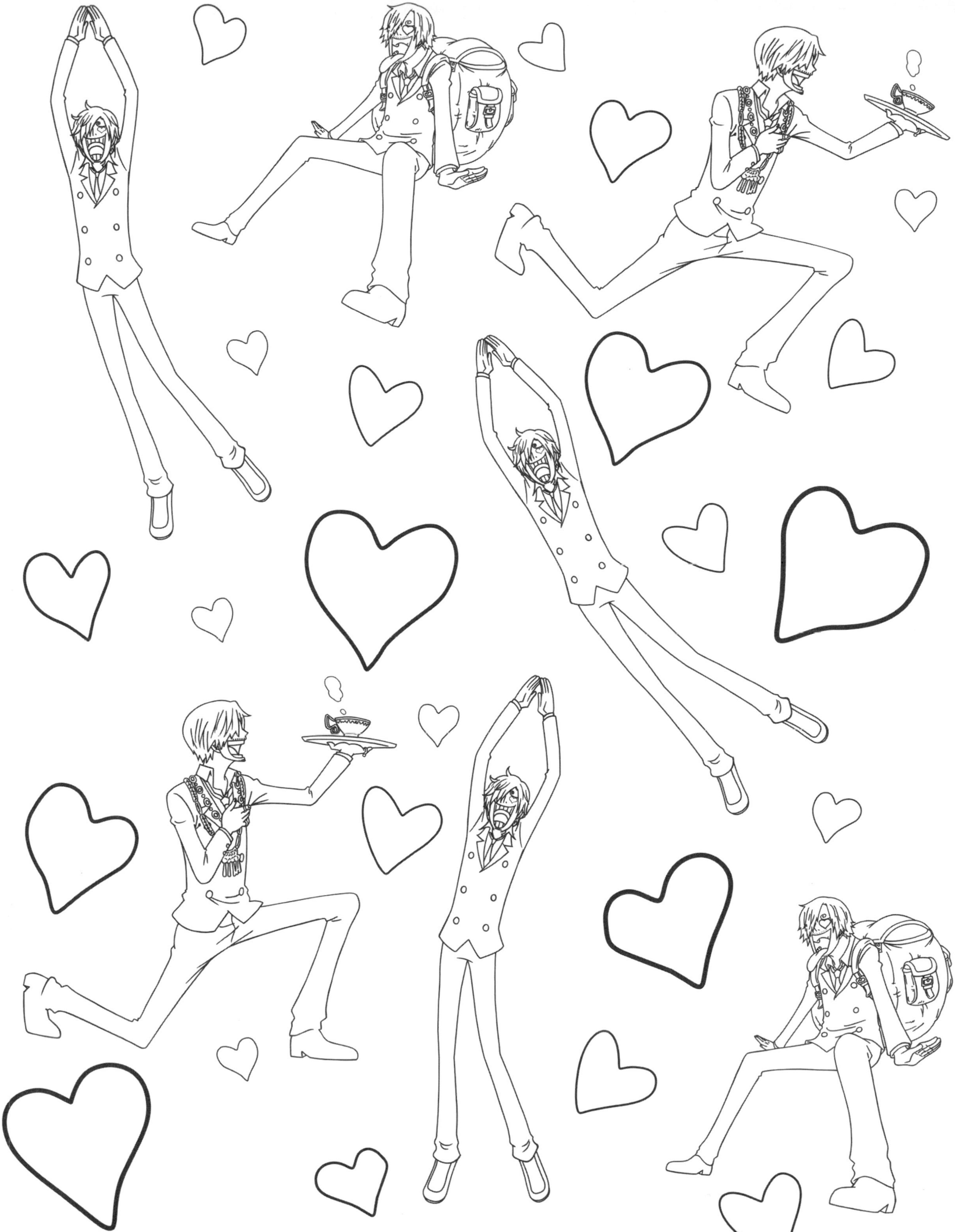

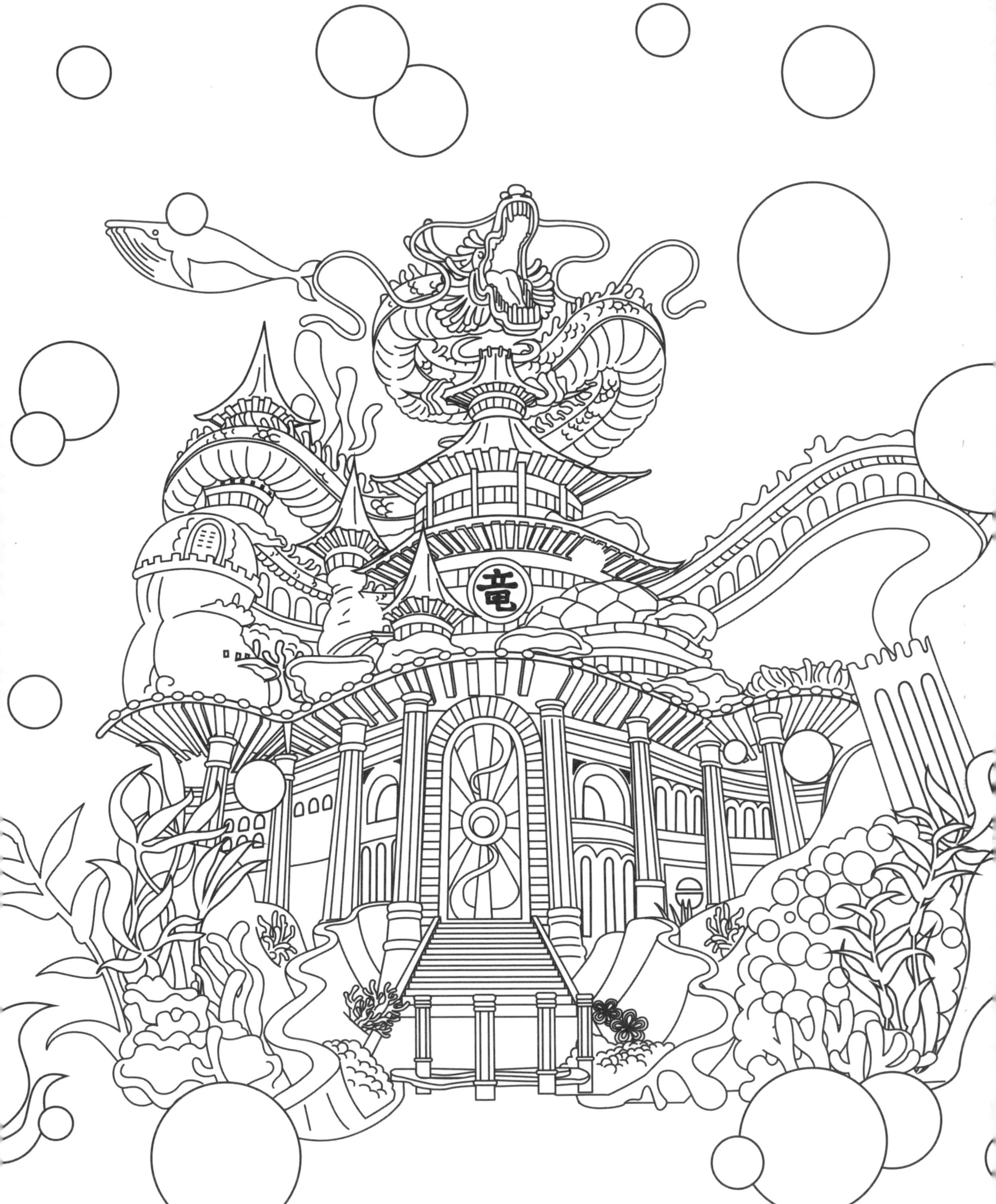
竜

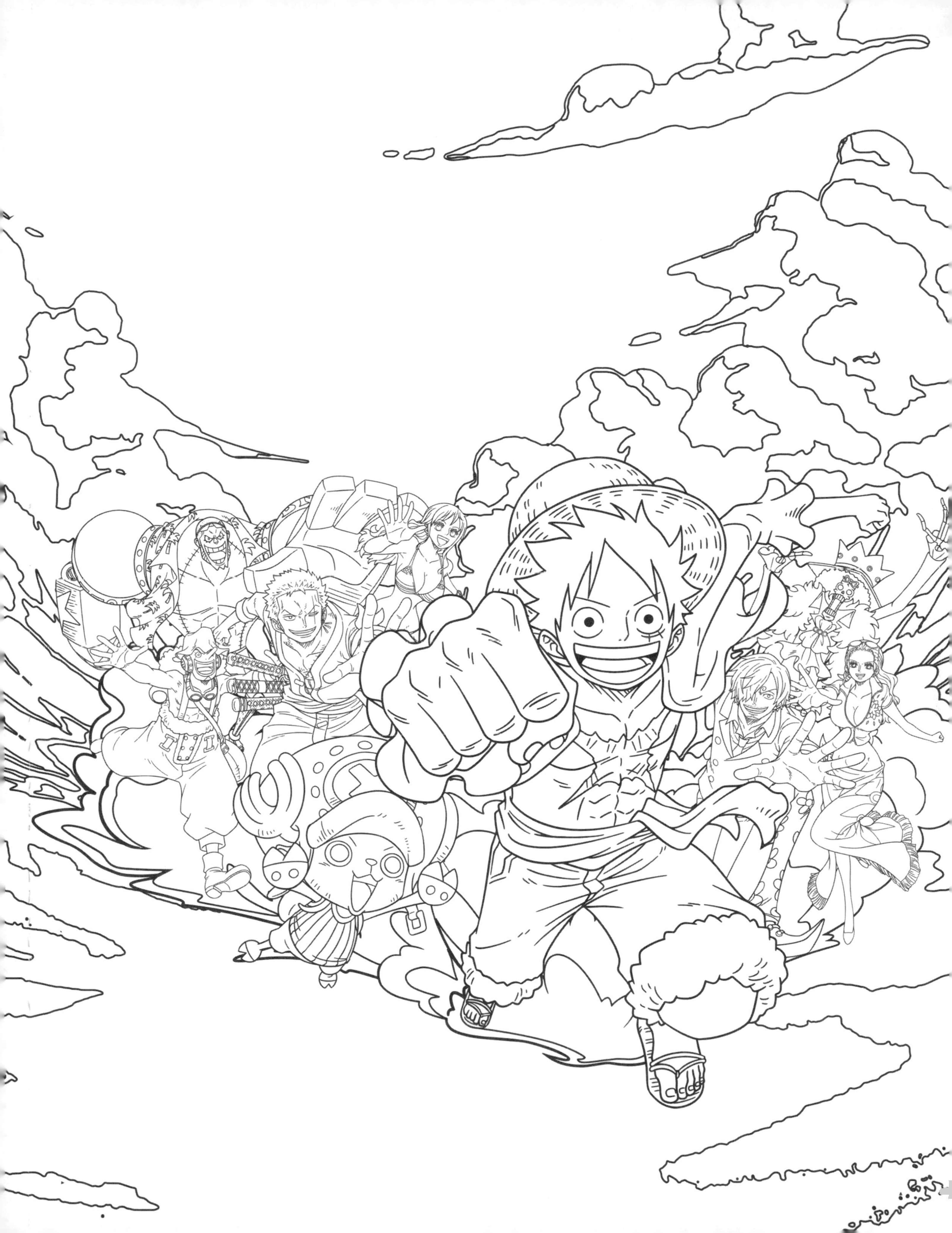

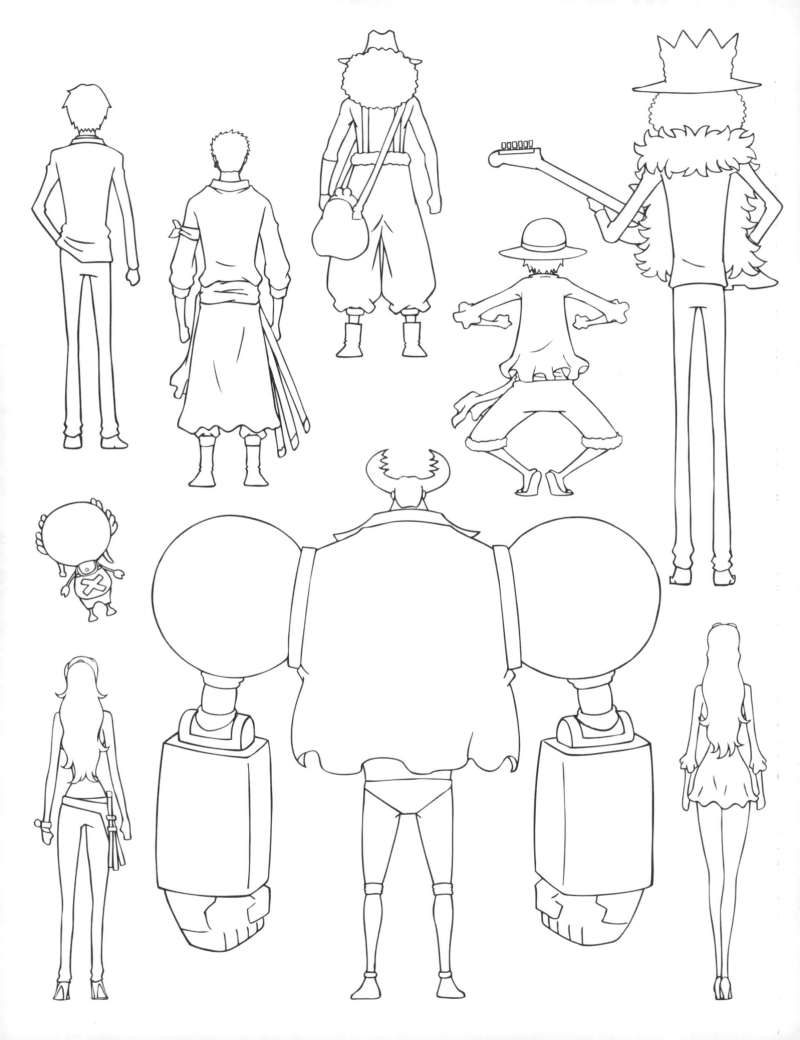

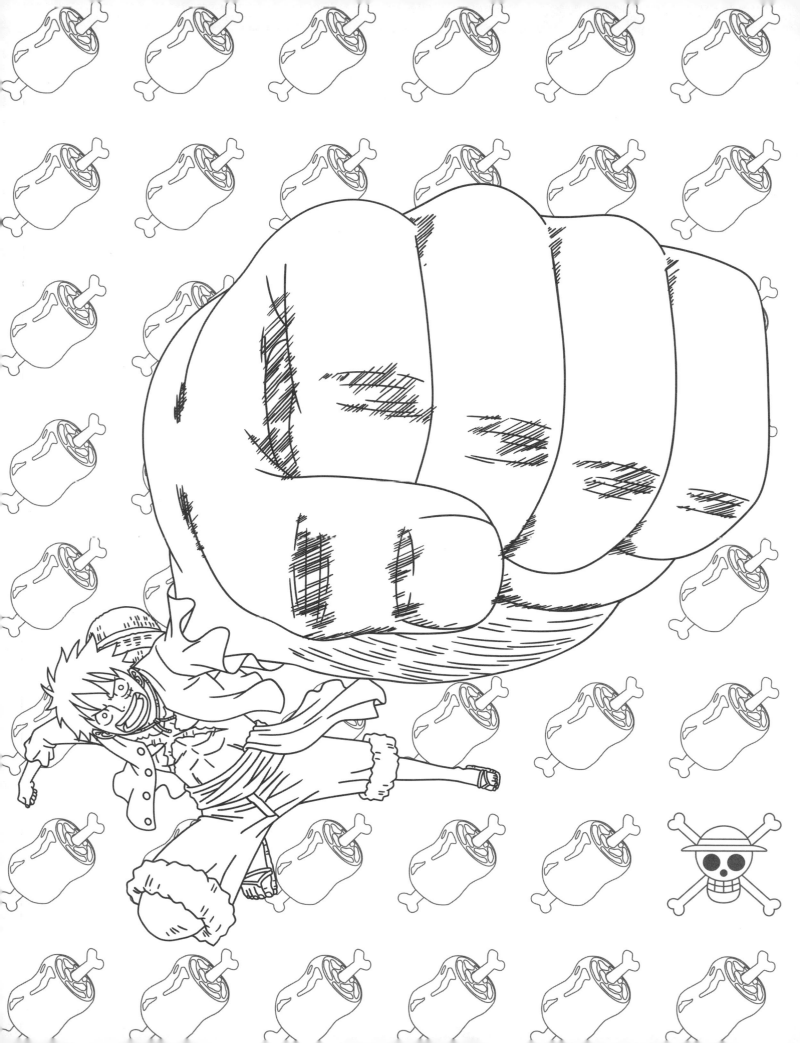

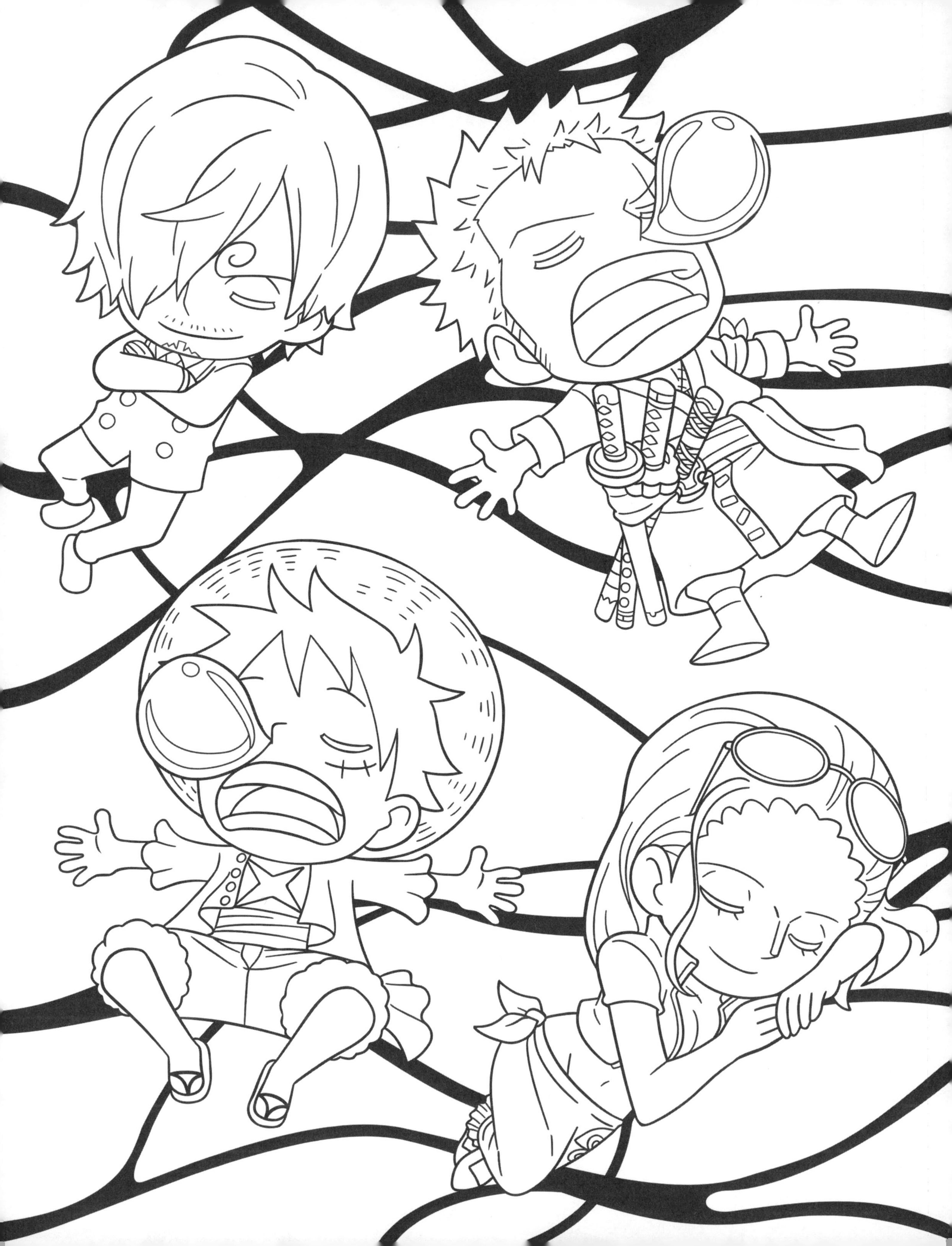

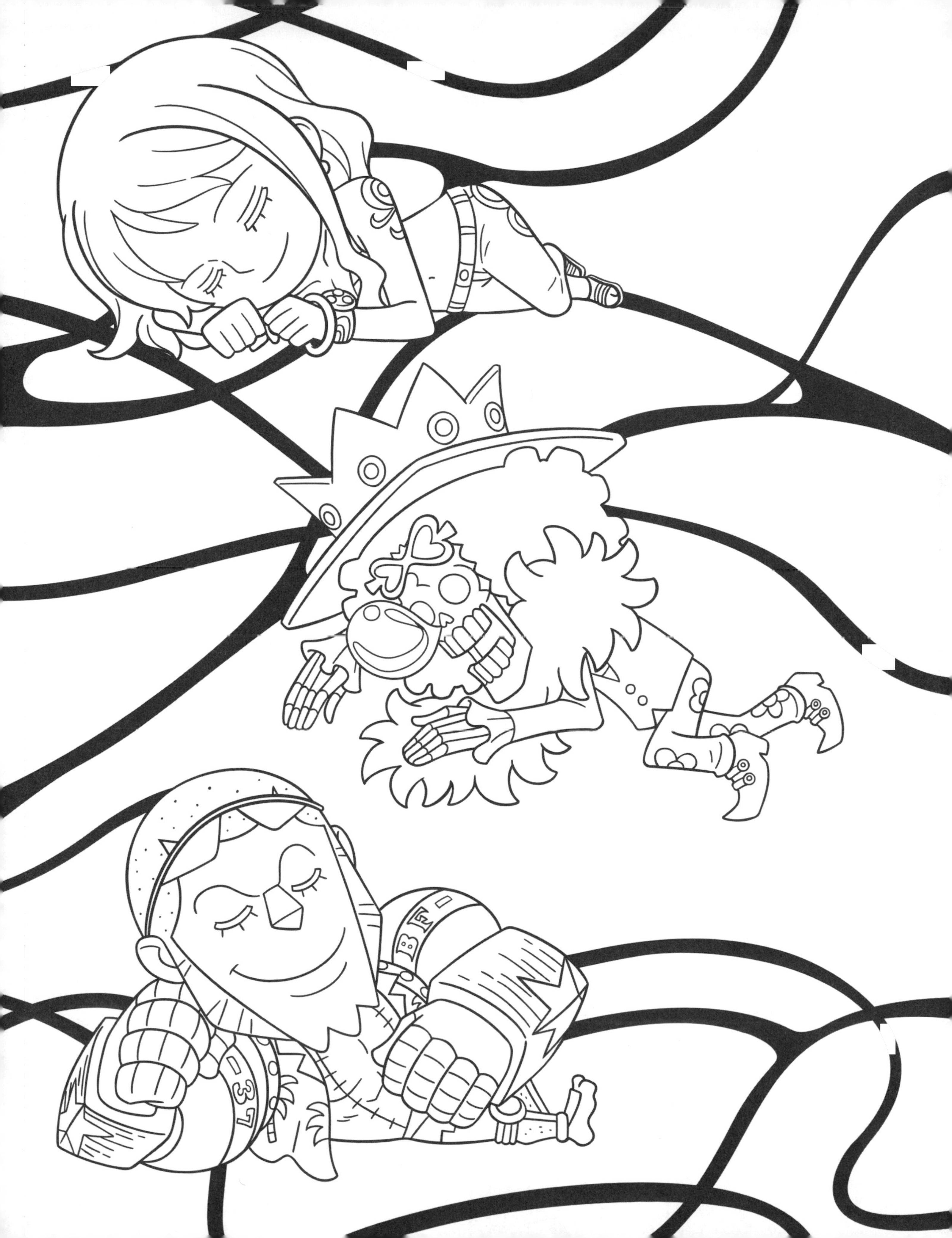

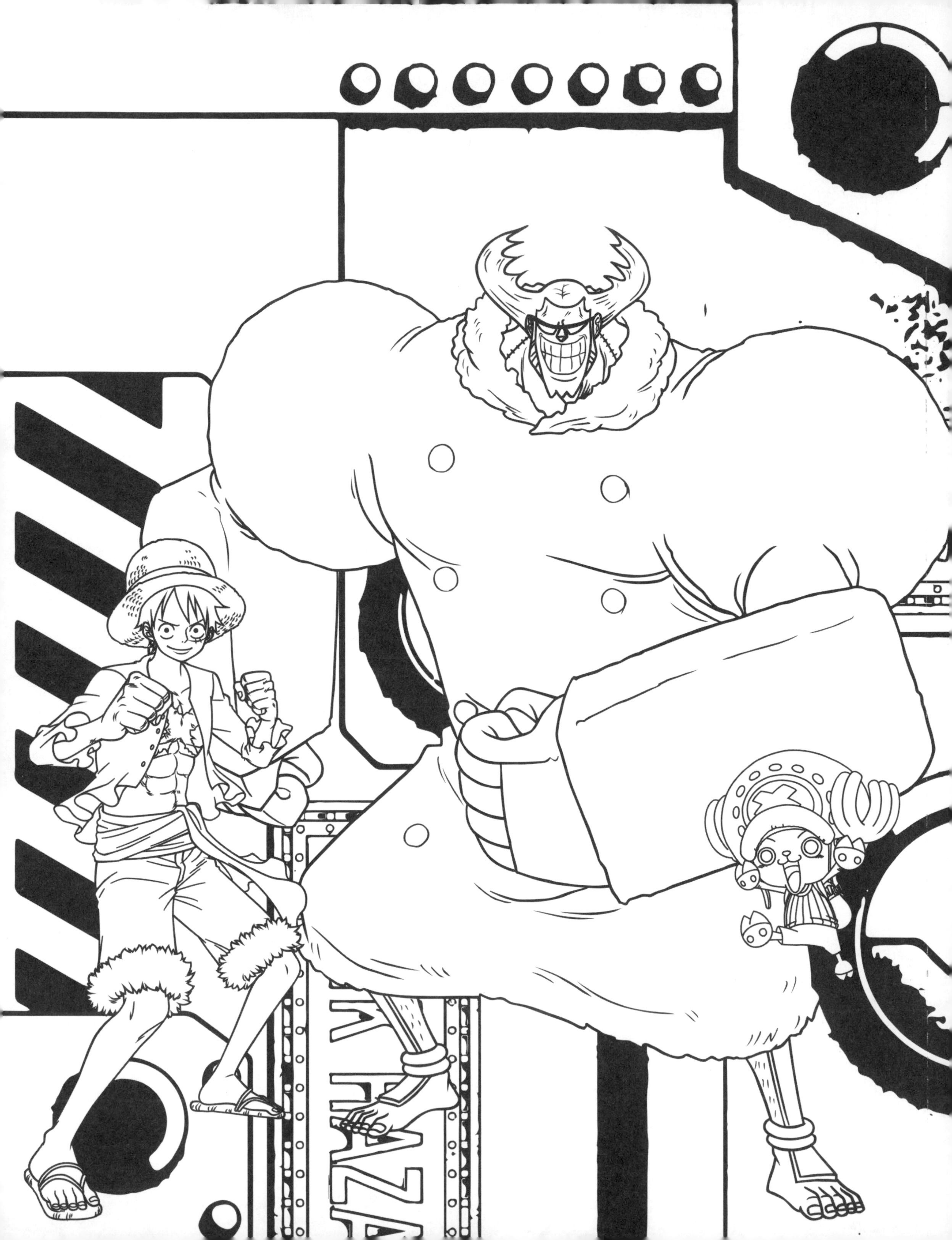

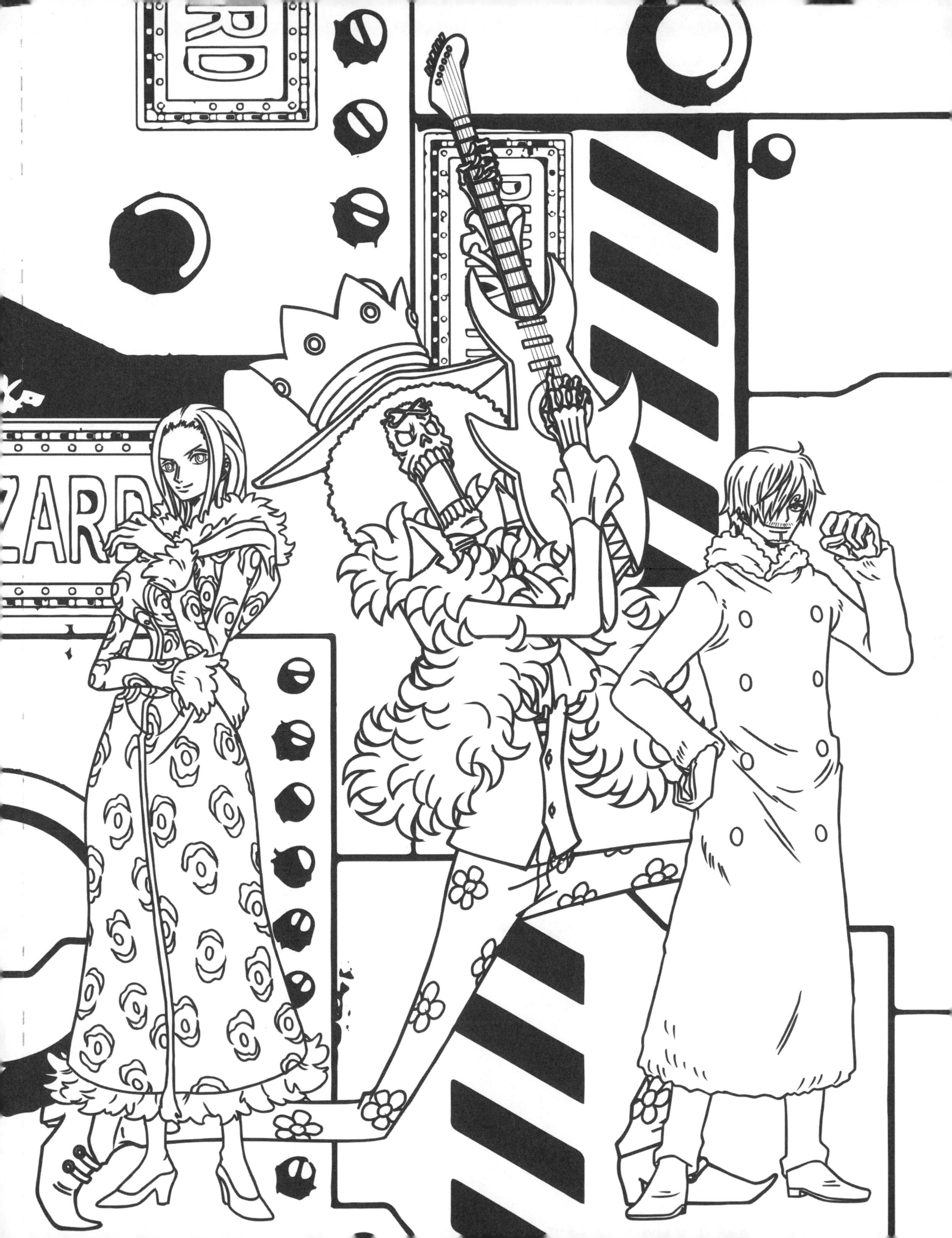
RD
ZARD

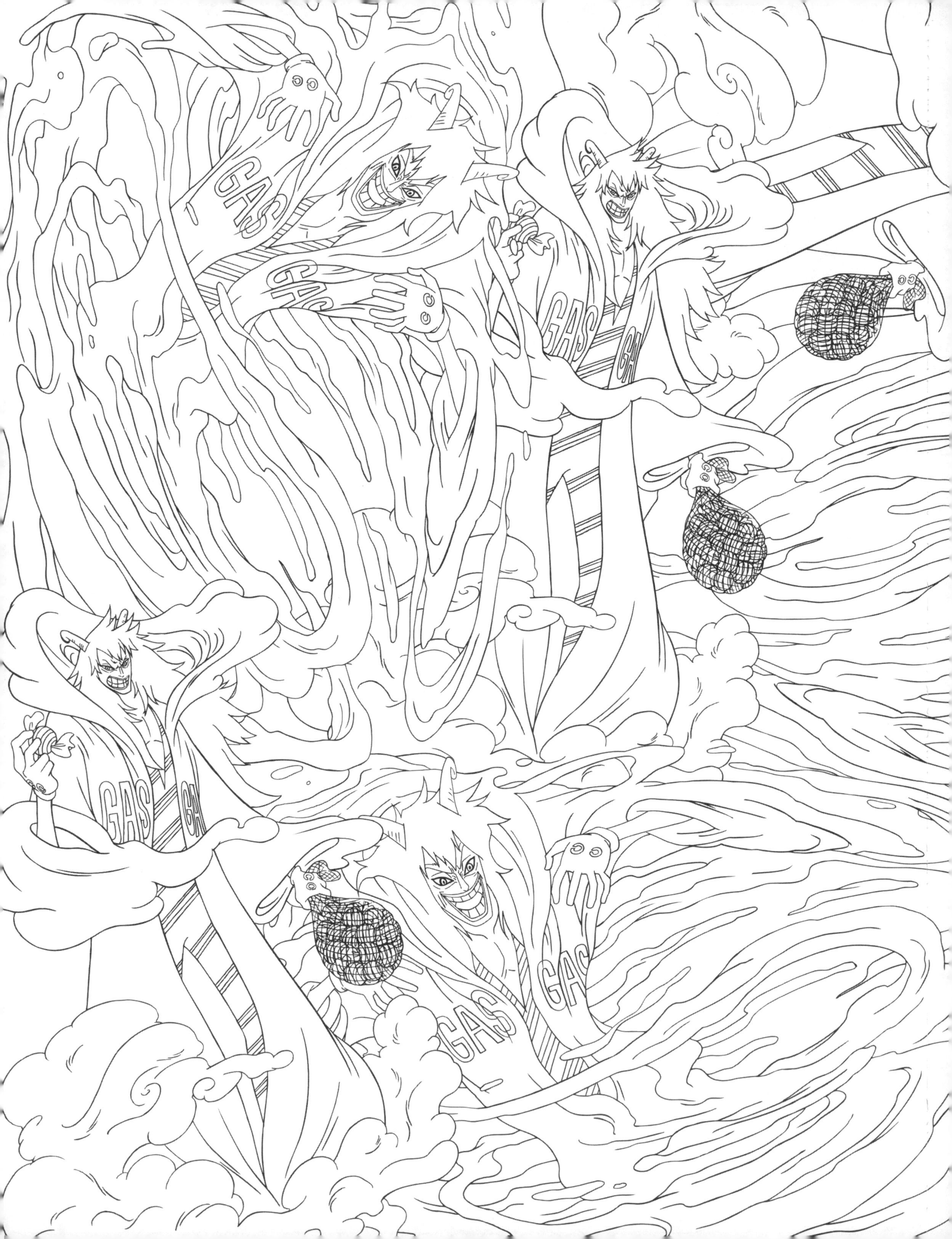
GAS
GAS
GAS
GAS
GAS

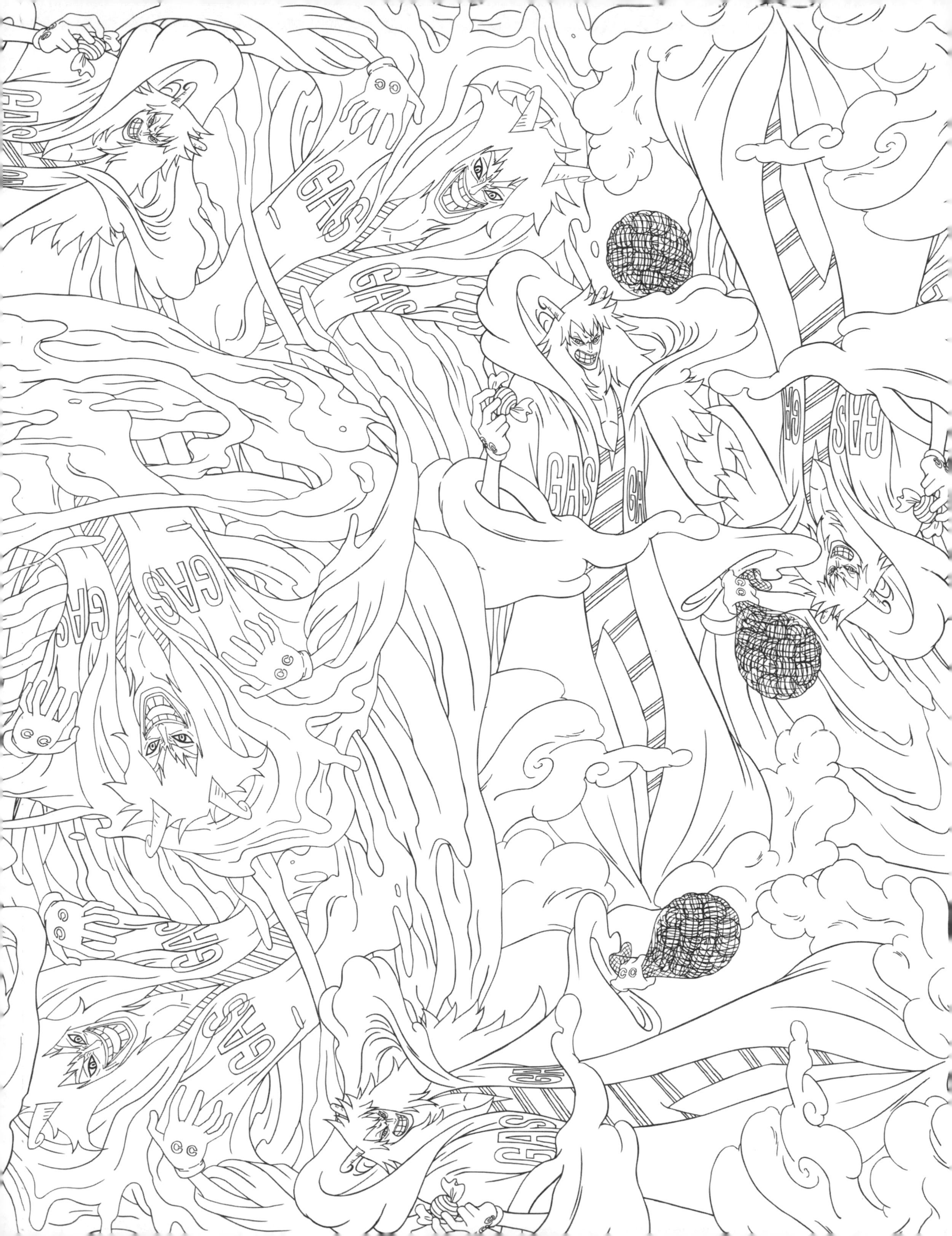
GAS
GAS

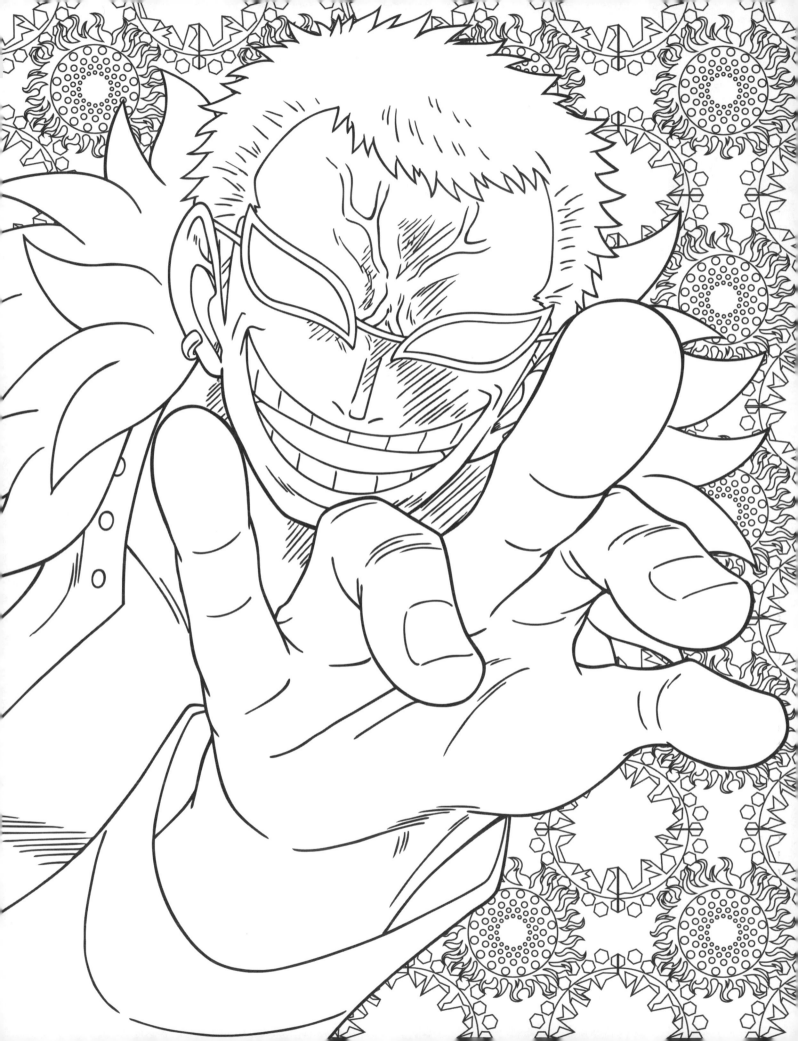

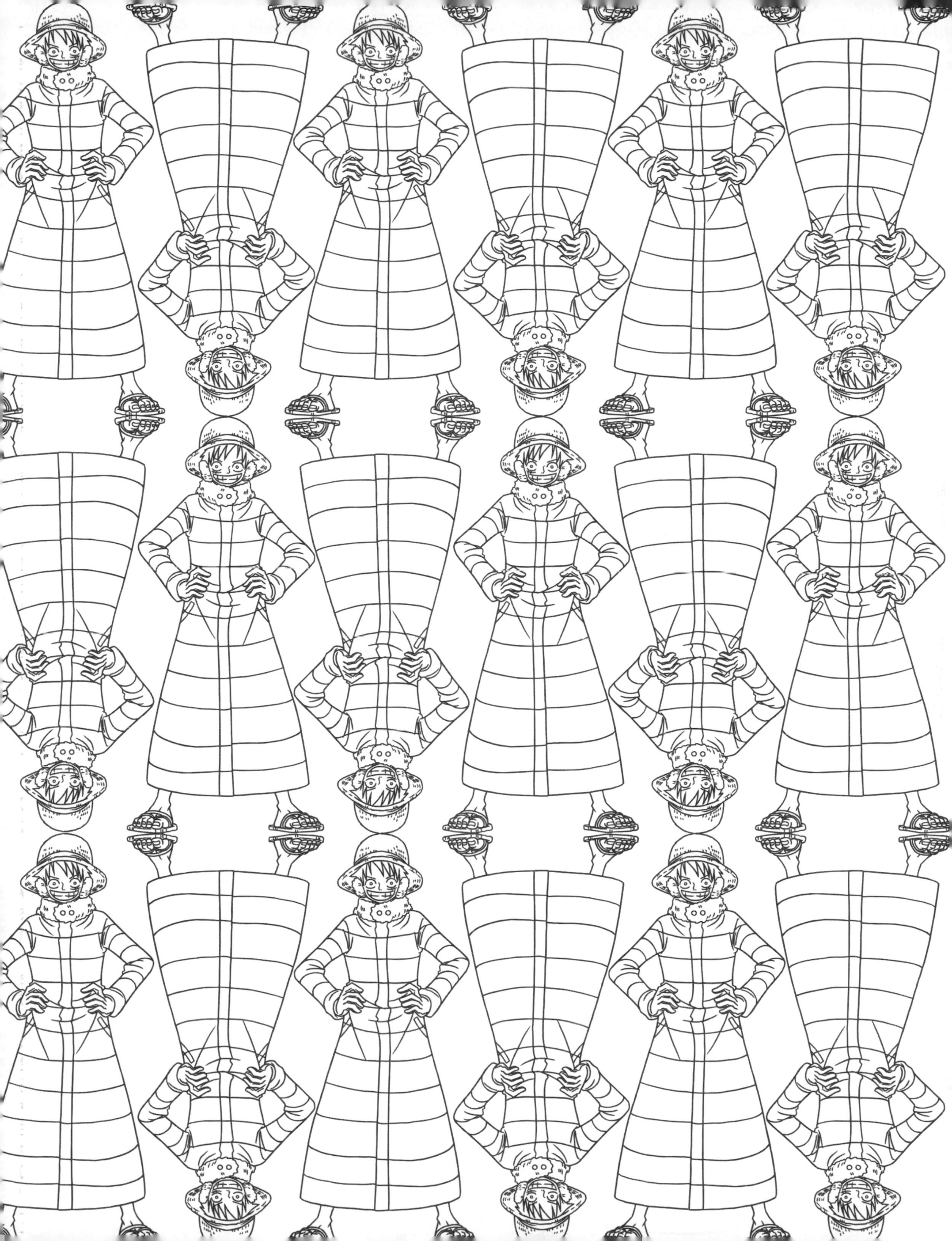

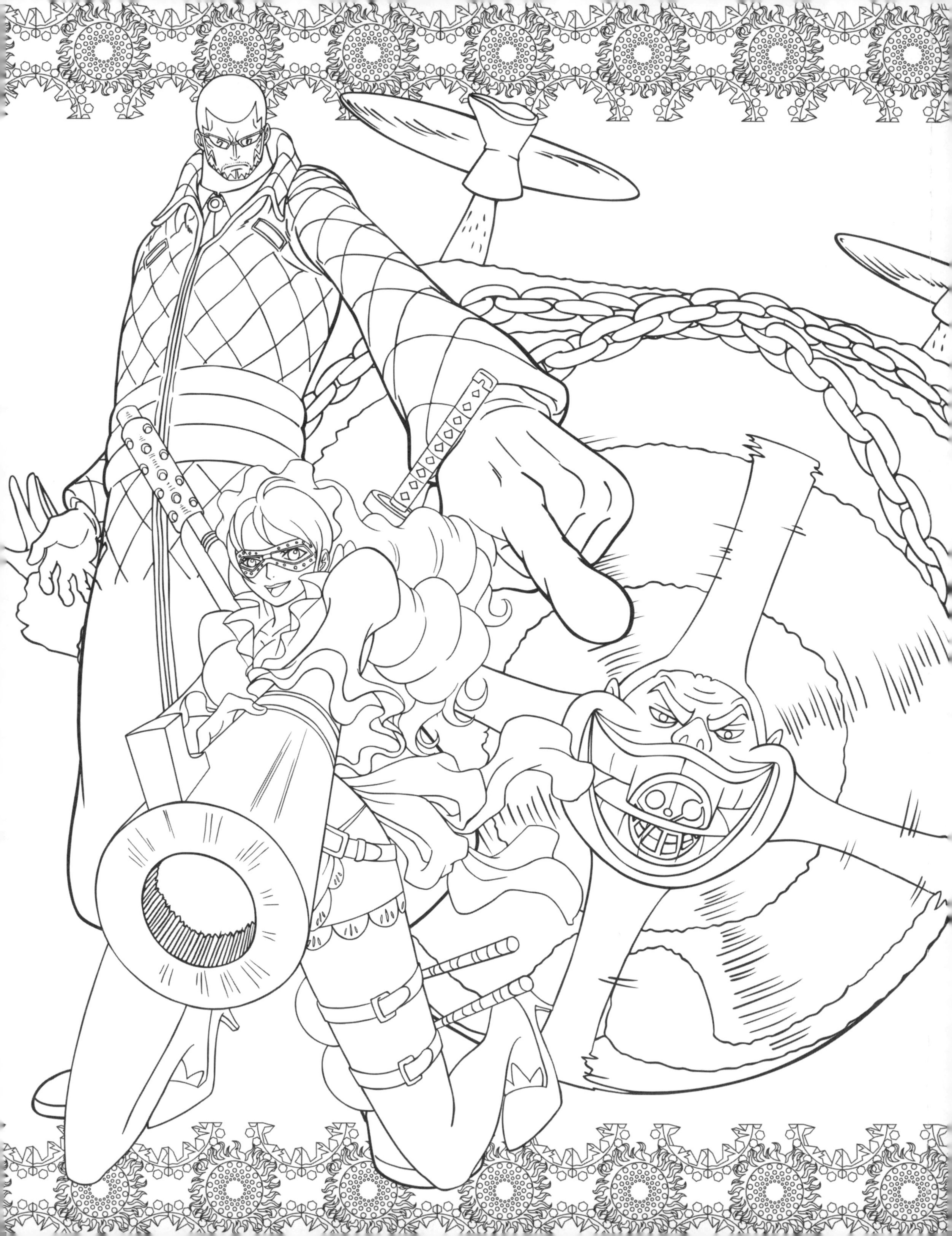

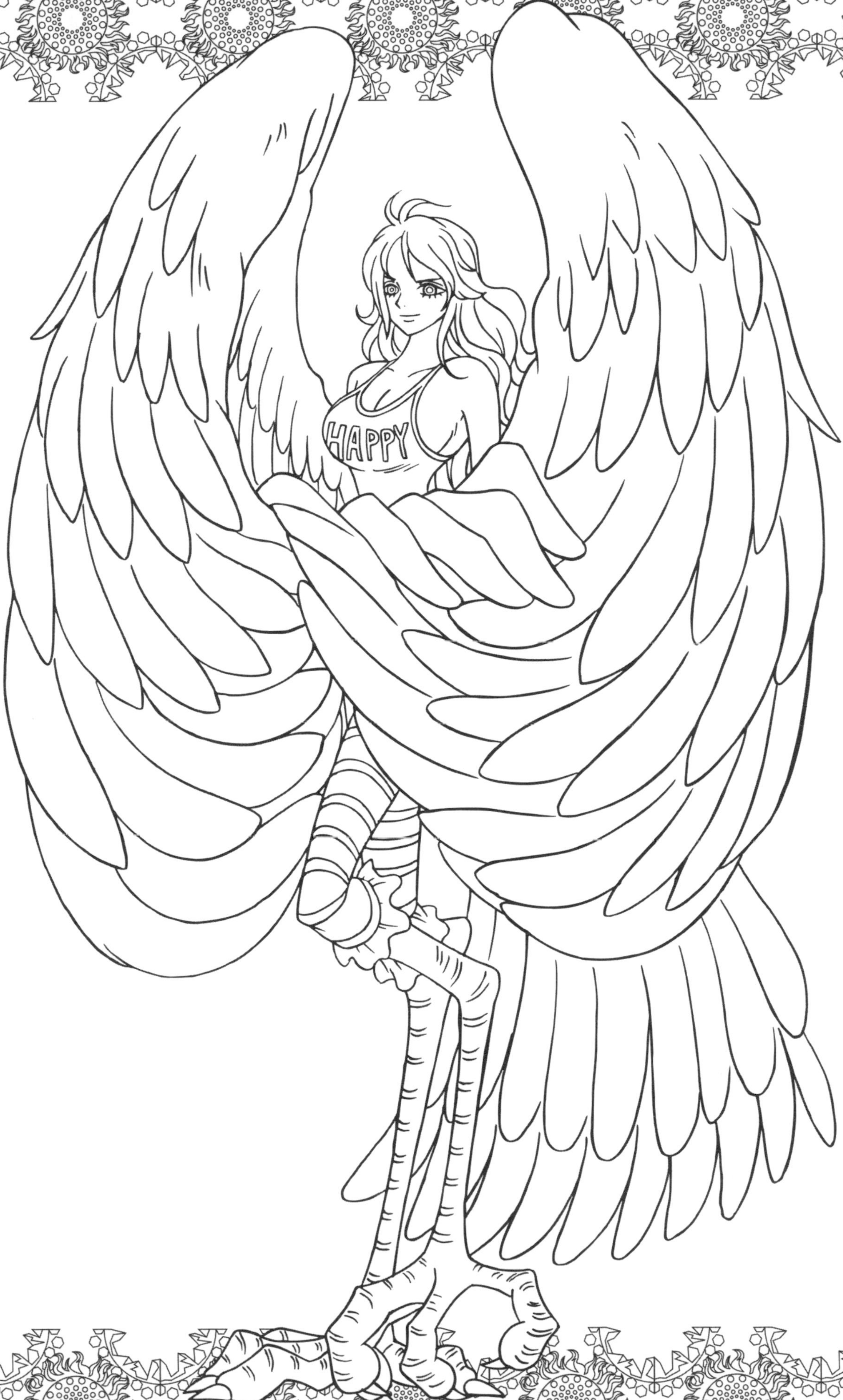
HAPPY

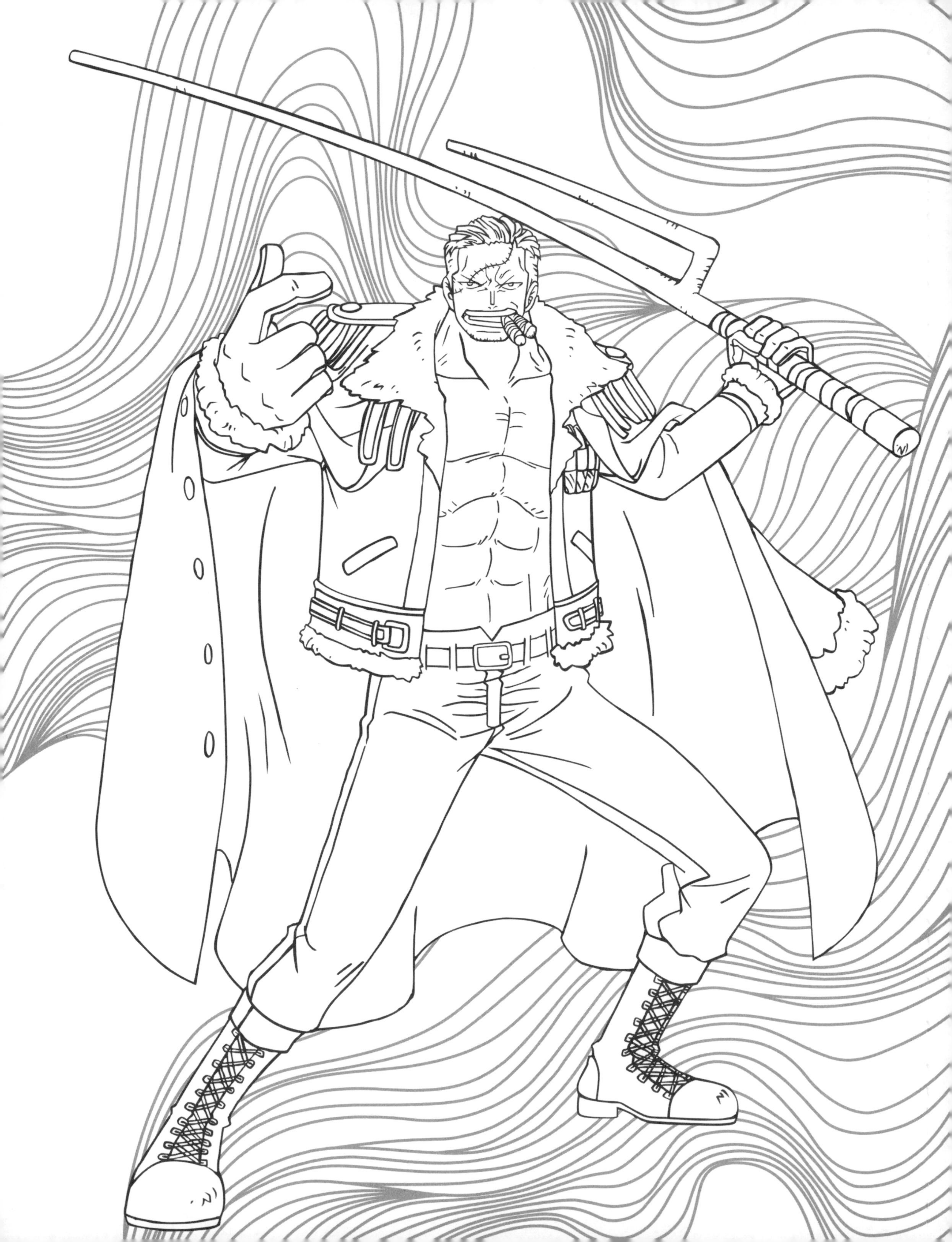

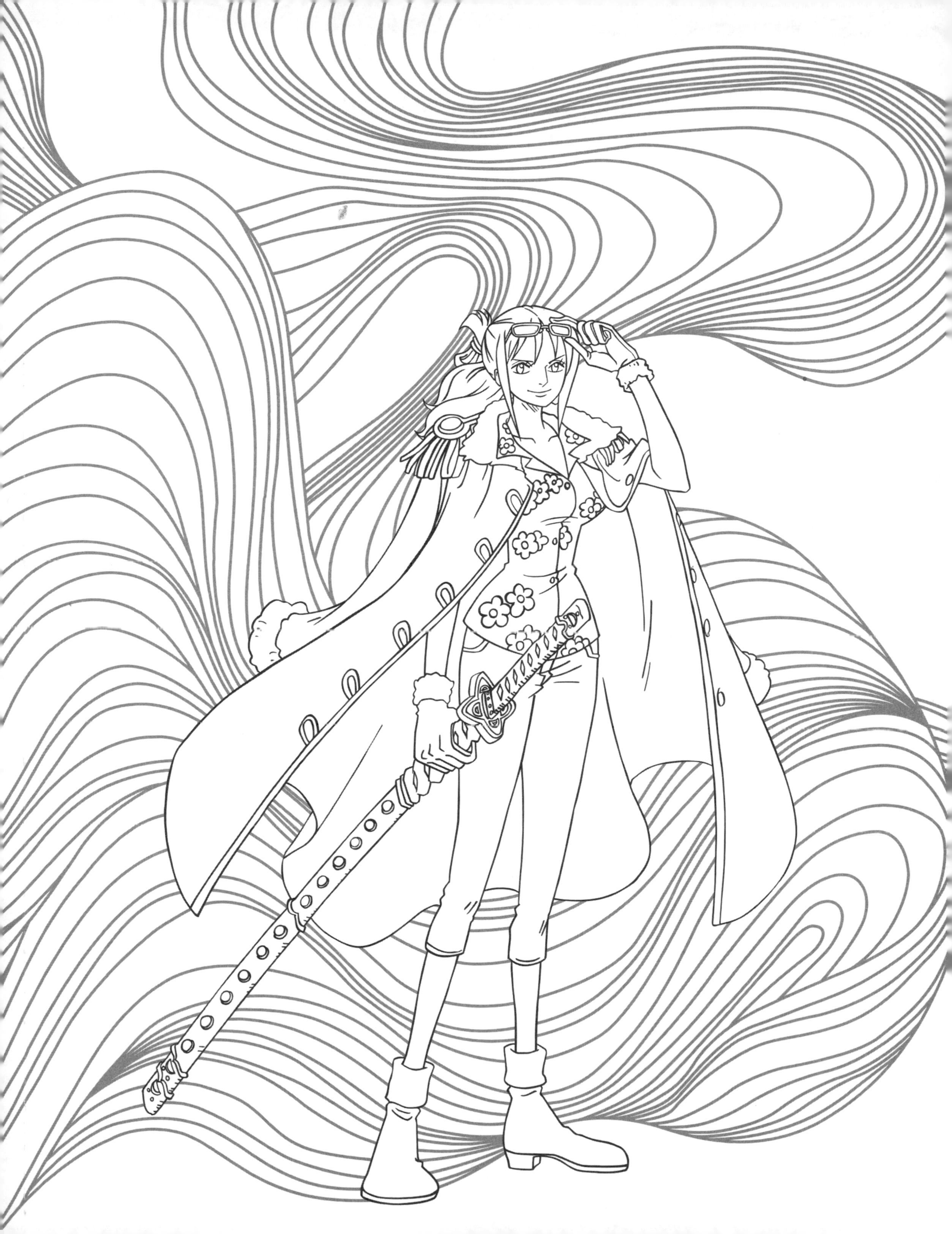

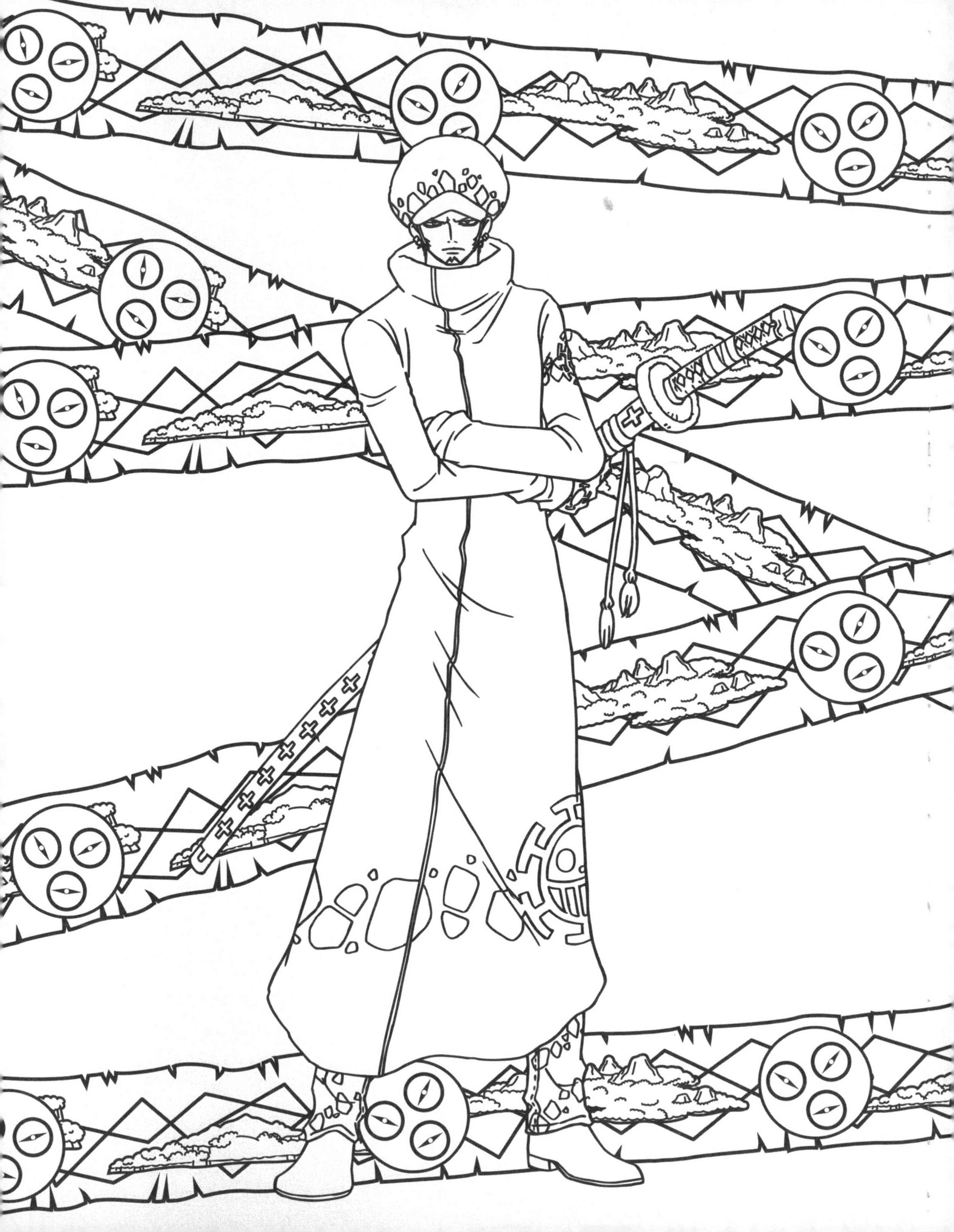

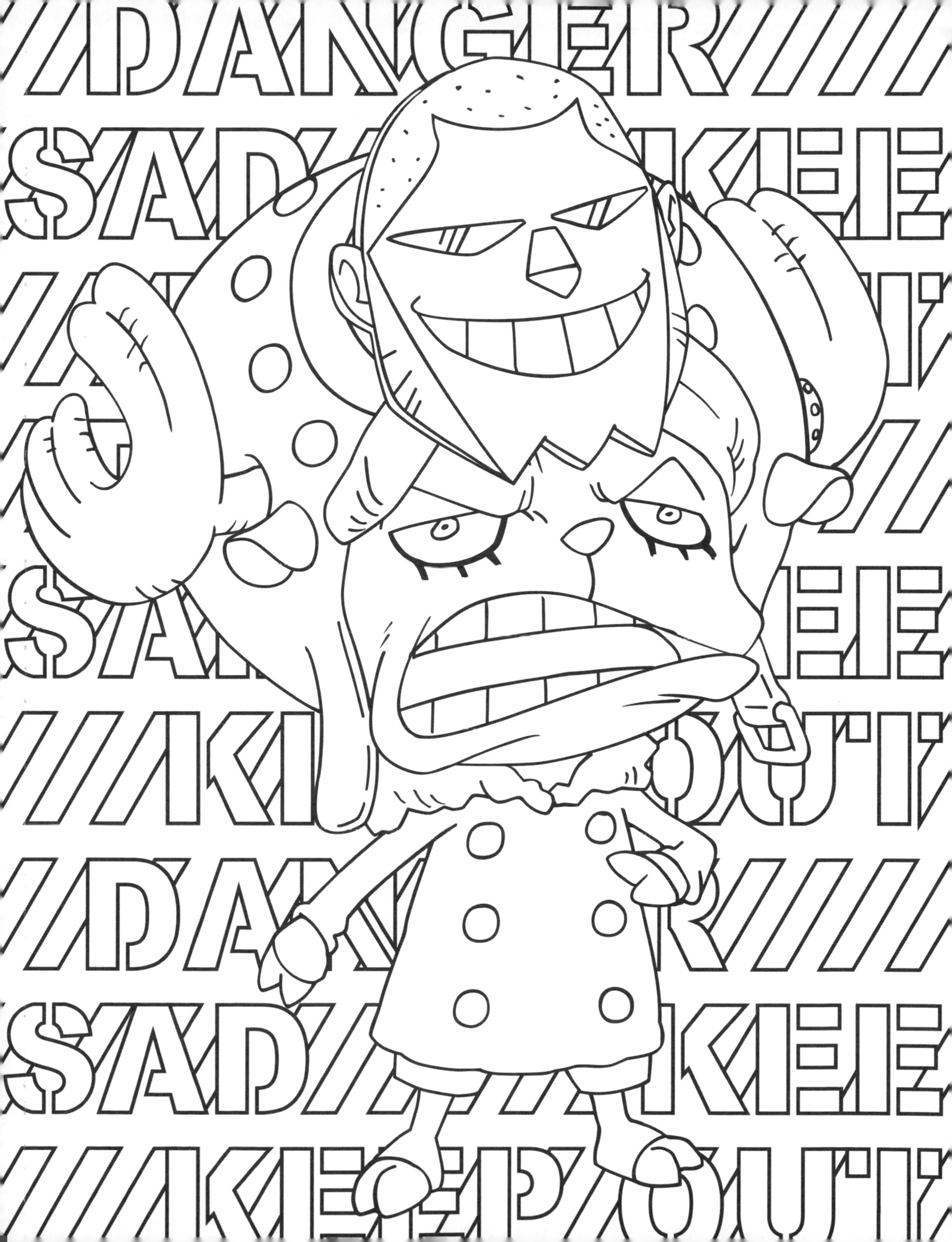
DANGER

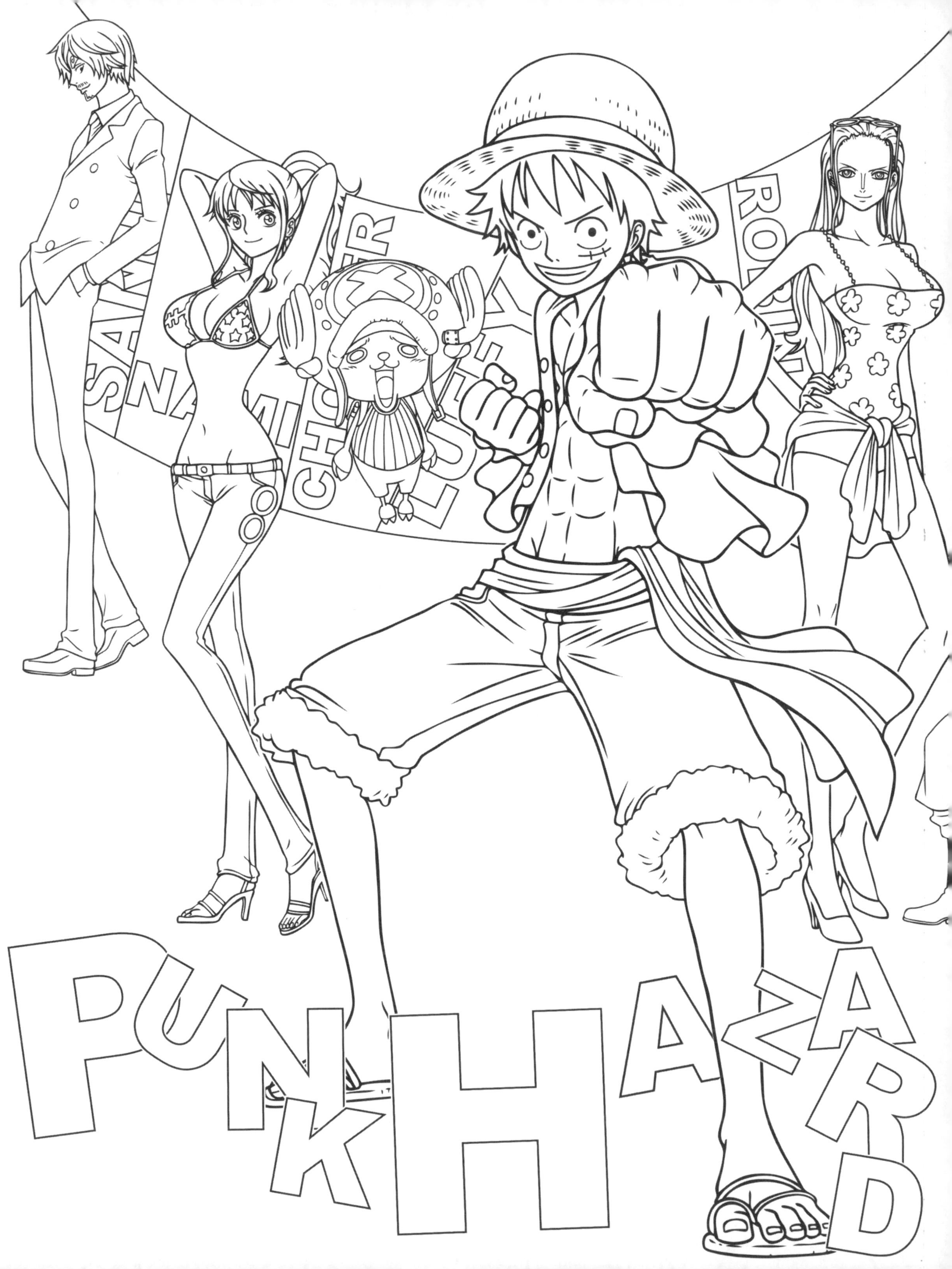
PUNK HAZARD

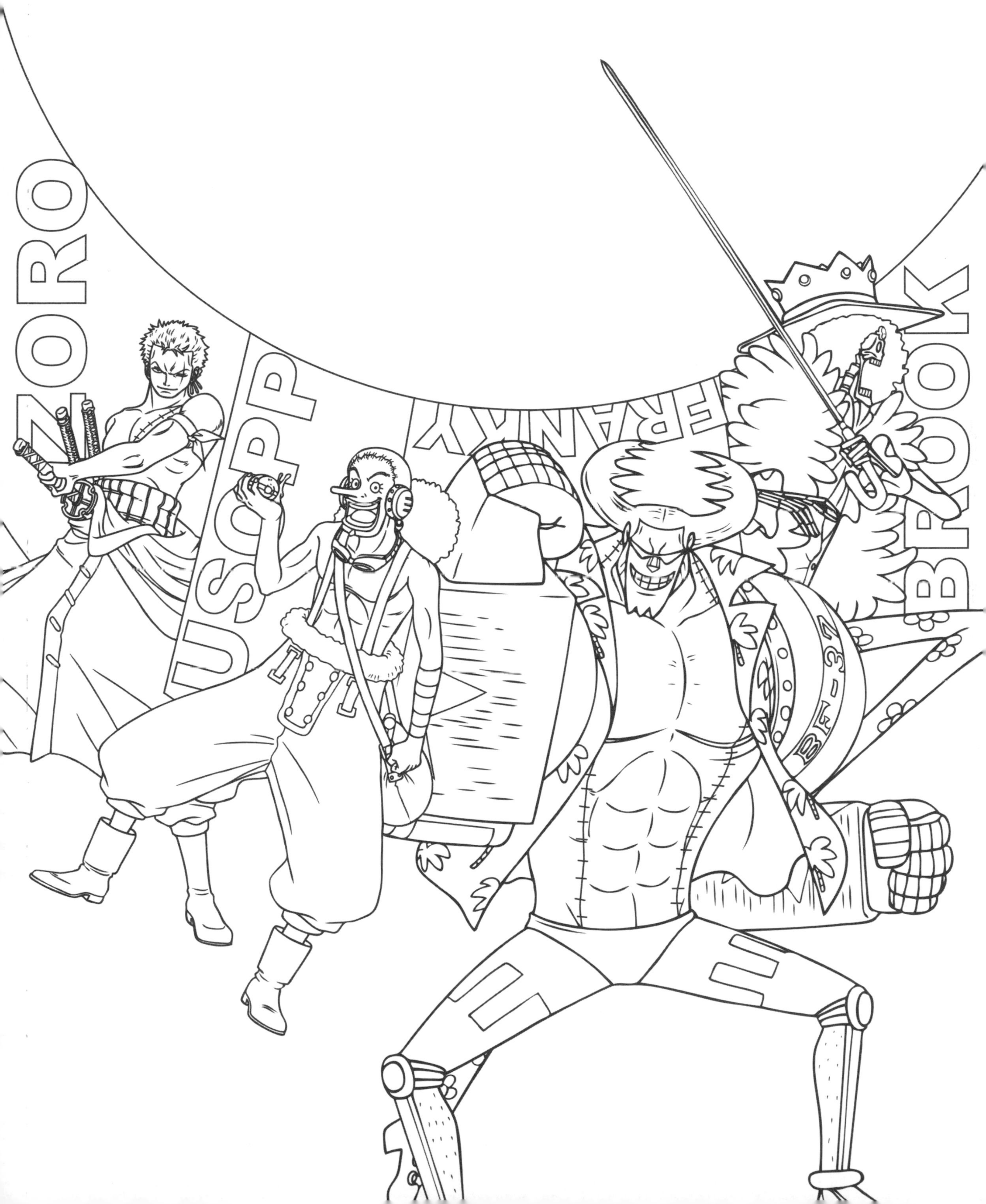
ZORO
USOPP
FRANKY
BROOK
BF-37

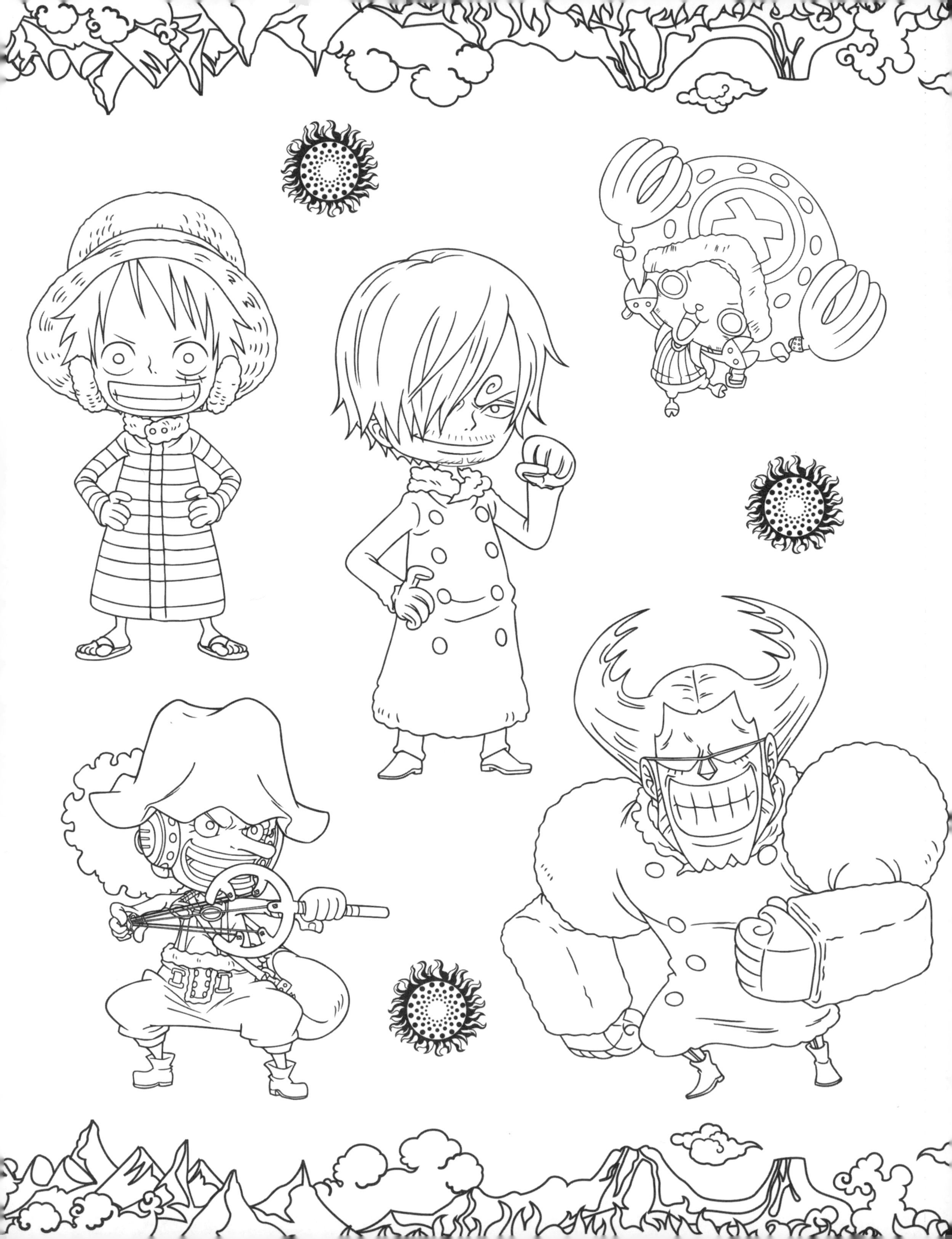

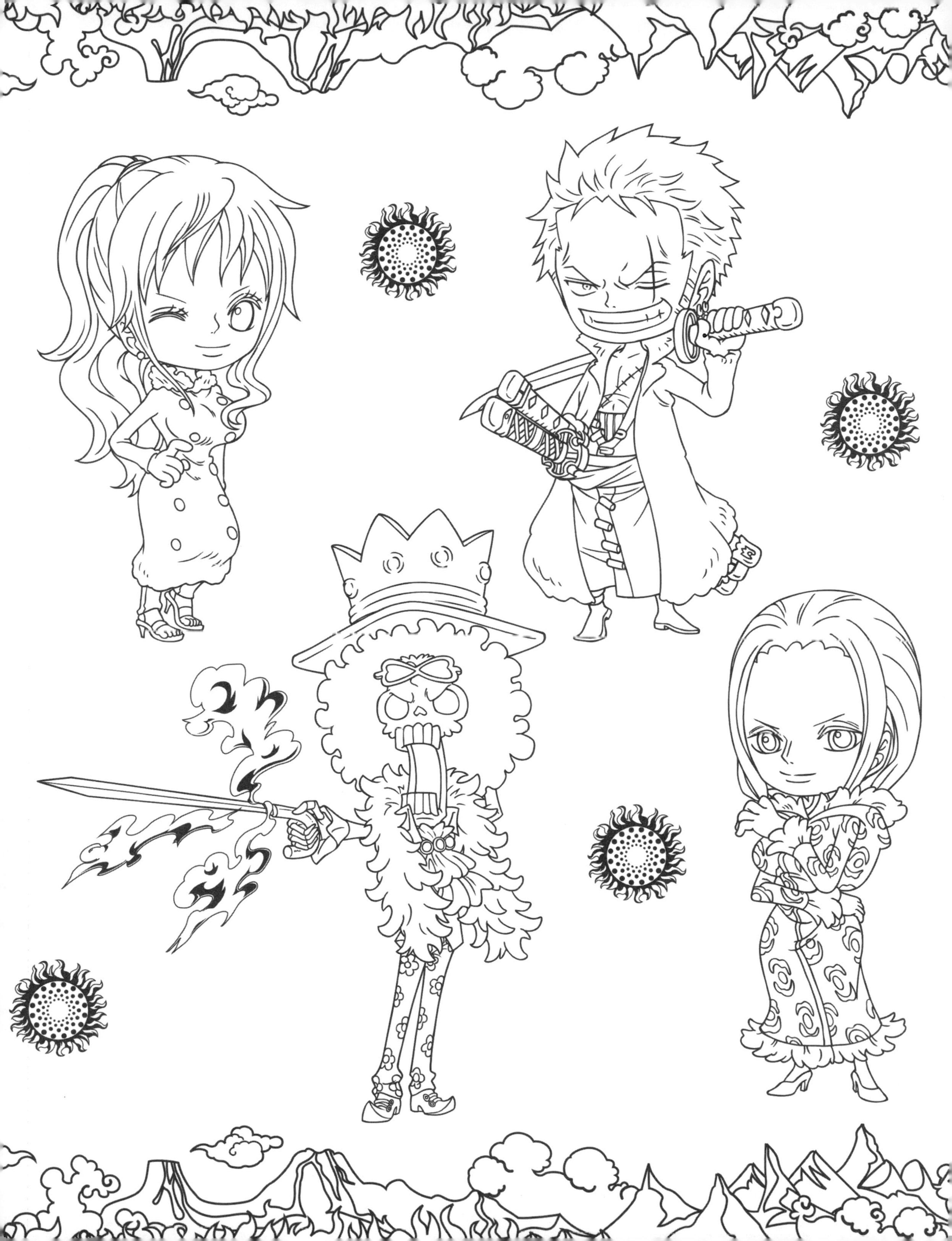

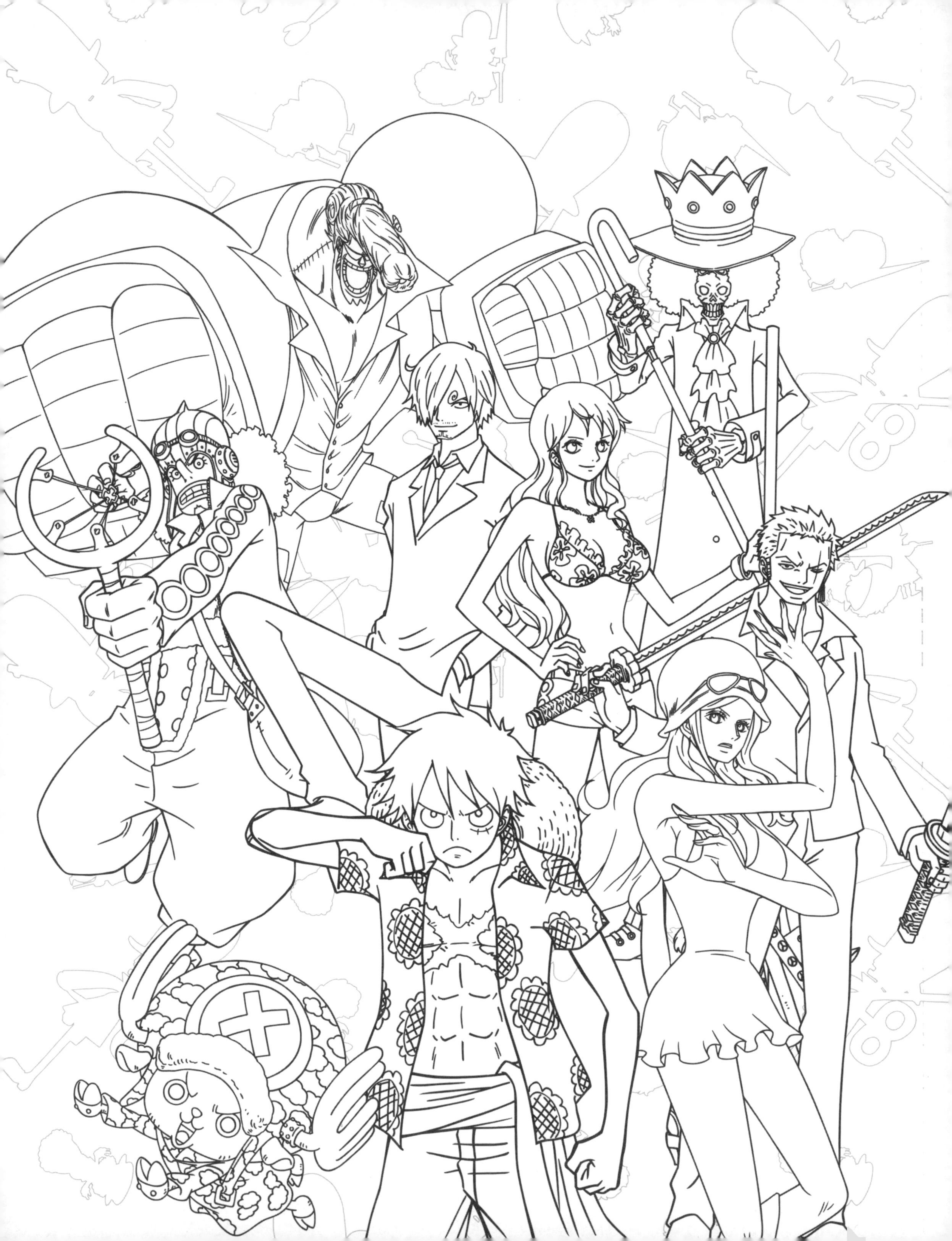

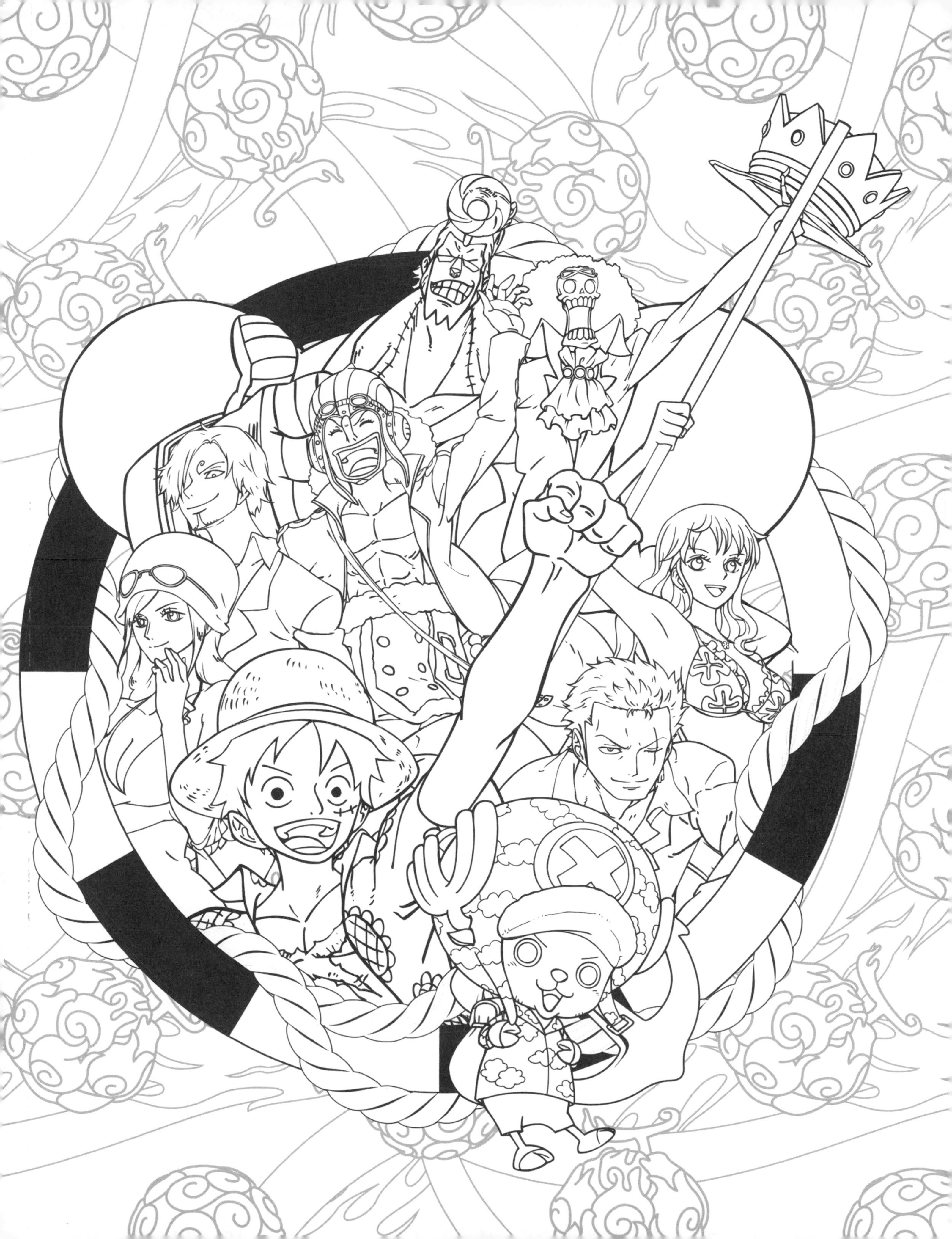

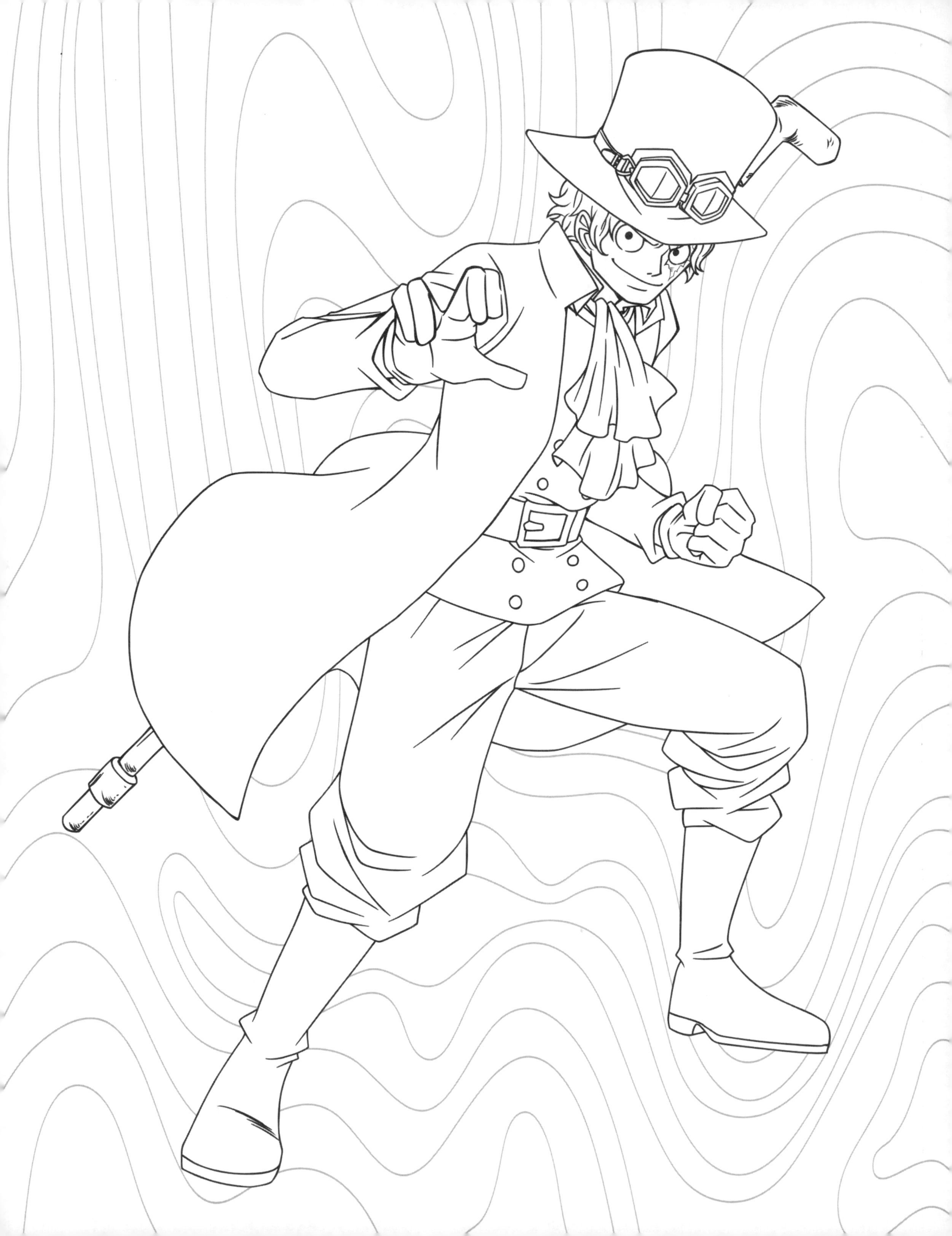

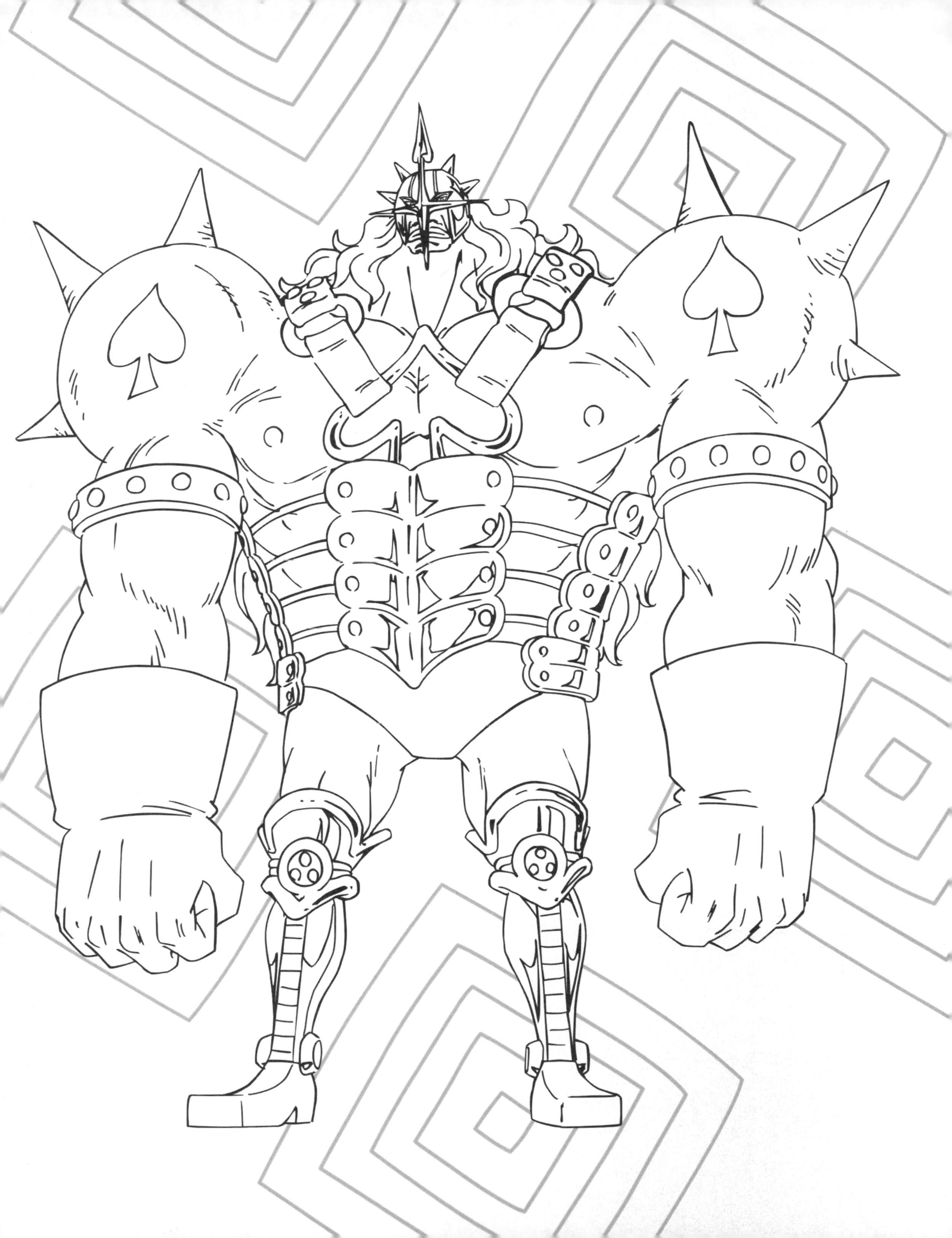

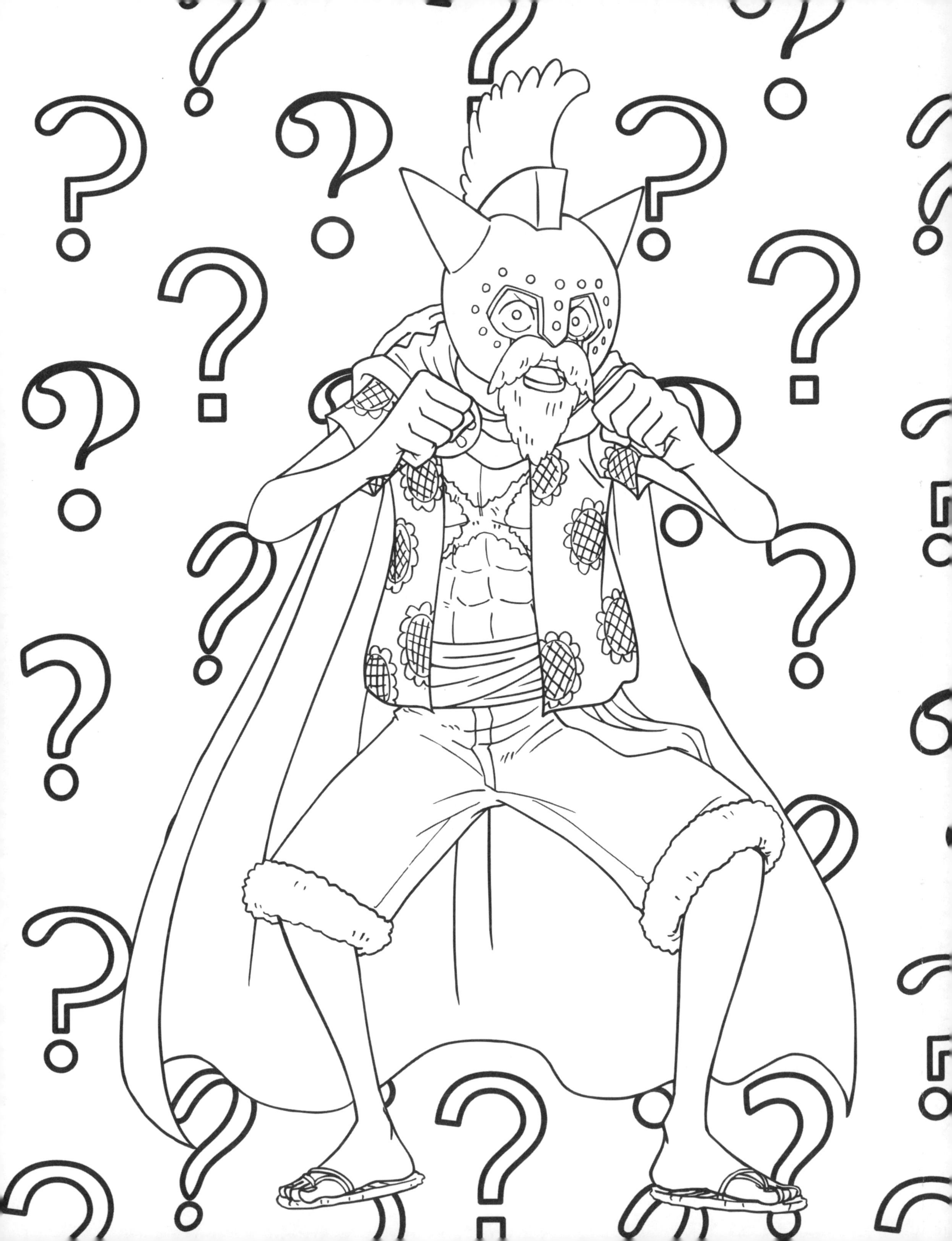

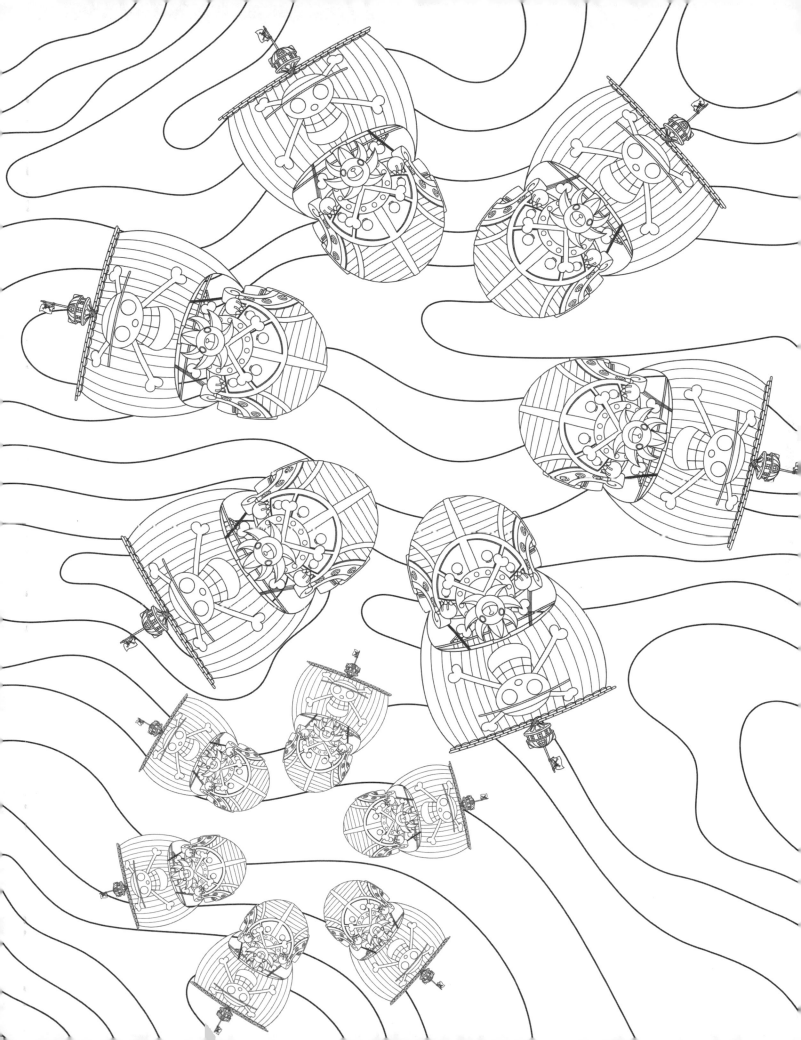

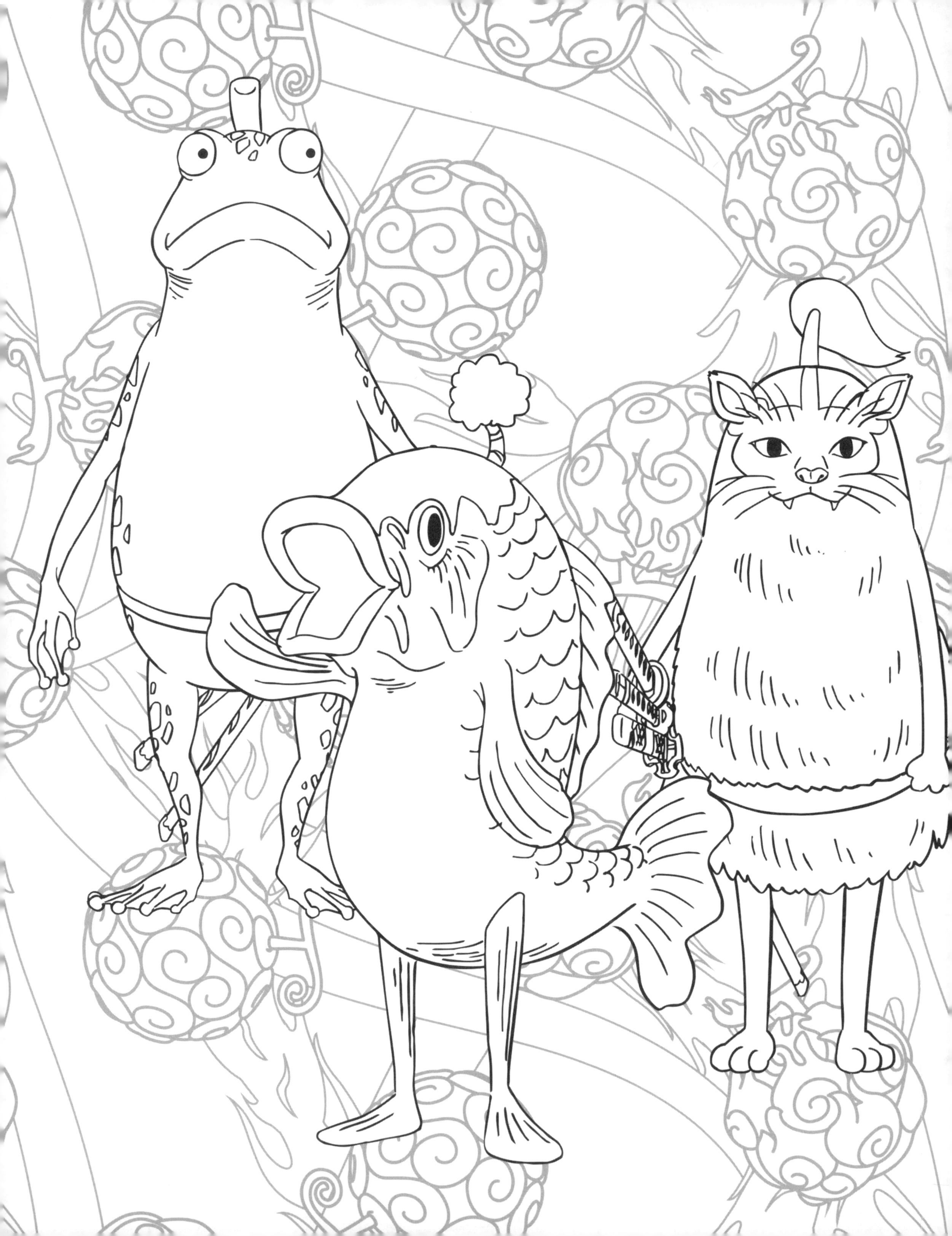

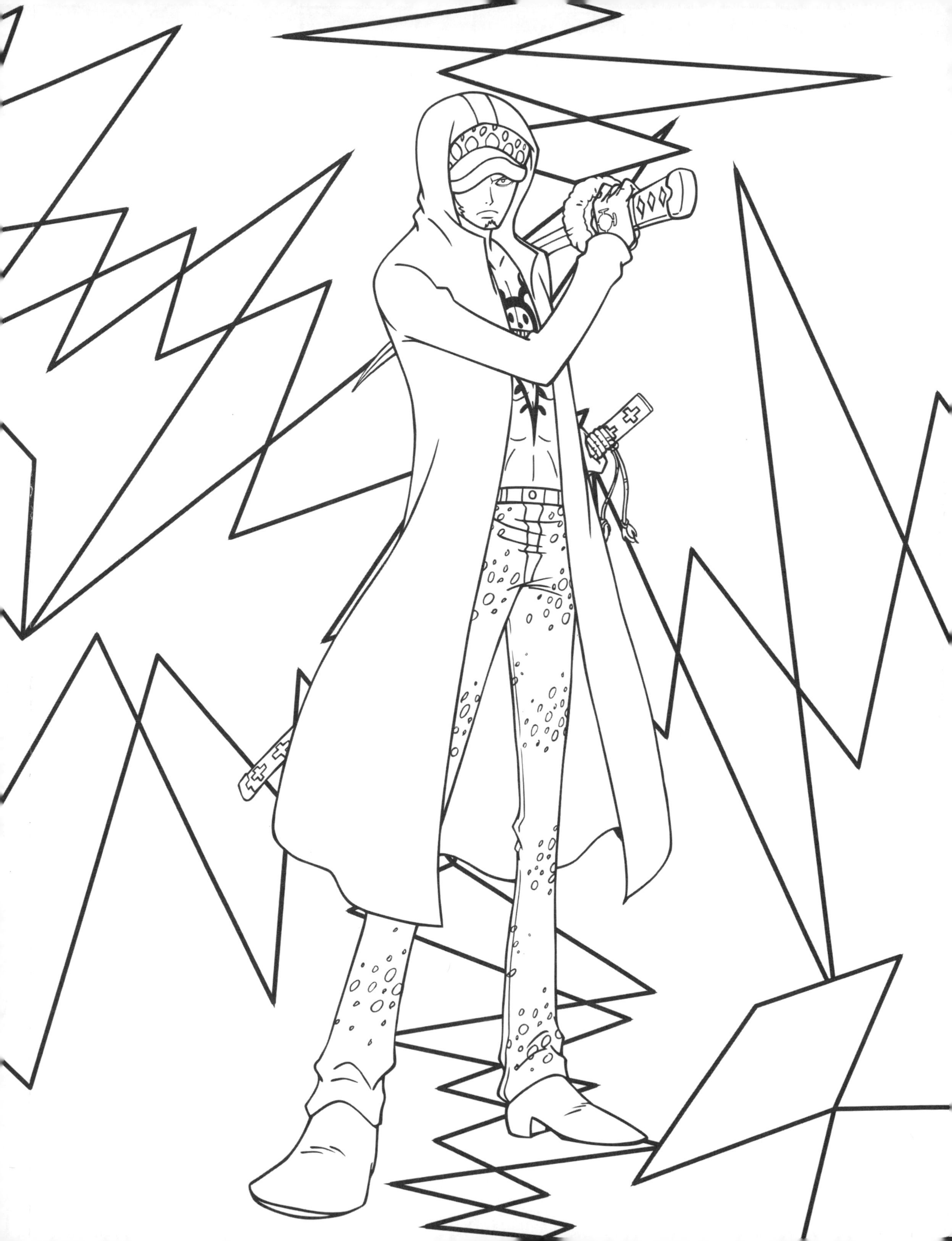

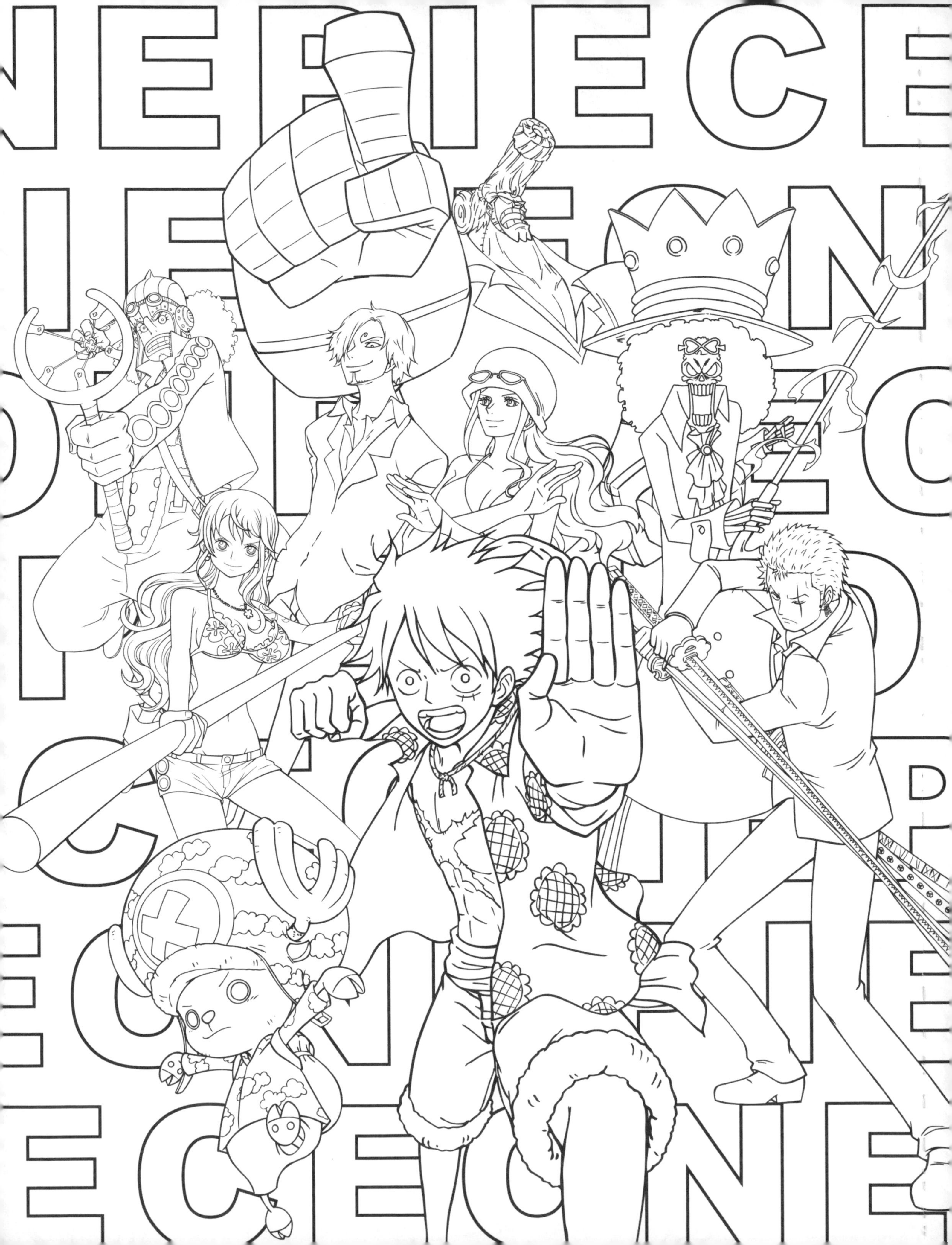

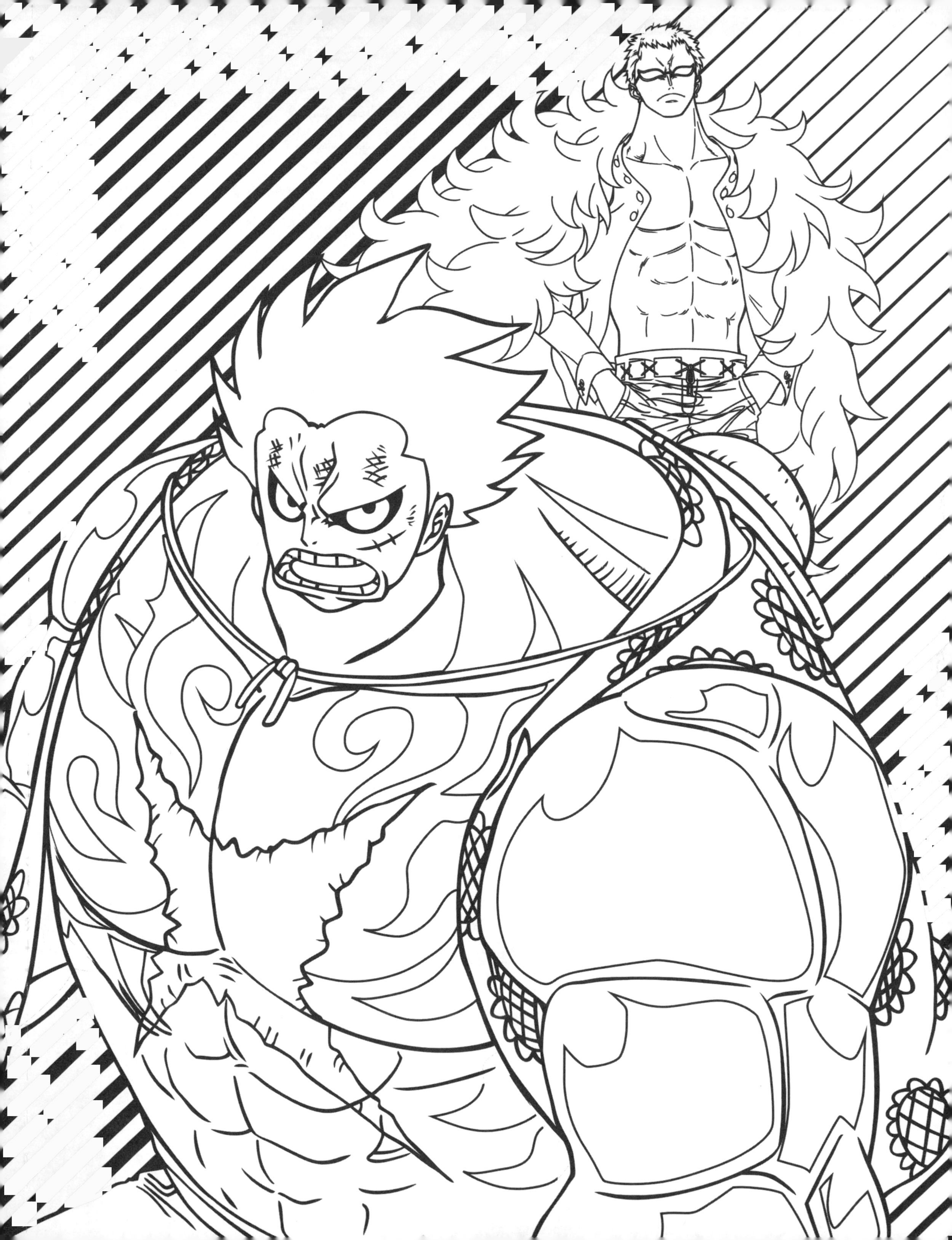

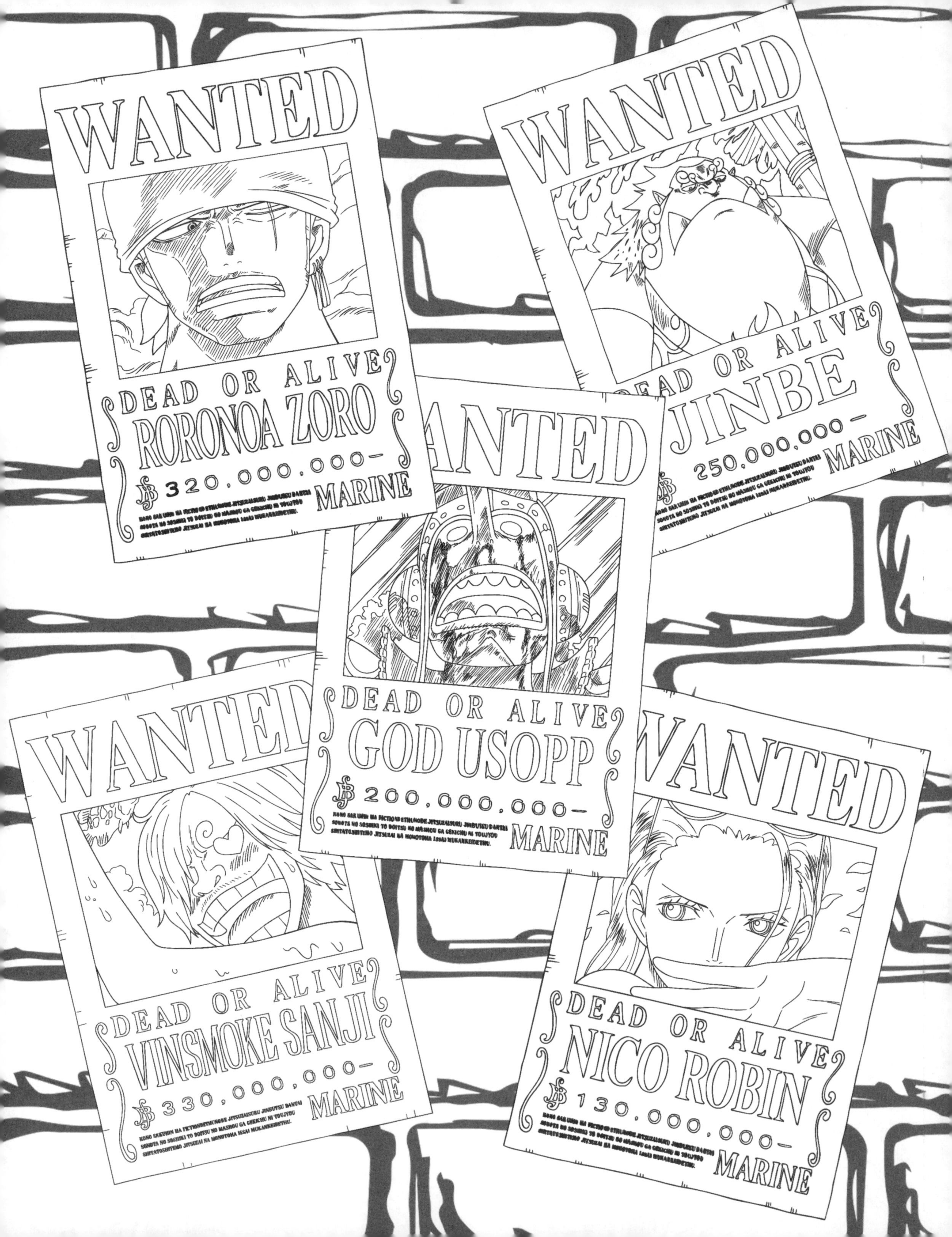
WANTED
DEAD OR ALIVE
RORONOA ZORO
320,000,000-
MARINE
WANTED
EAD OR ALIVE
JINBE
250,000,000-
MARINE
ANTED
DEAD OR ALIVE
GOD USOPP
200,000,000-
MARINE
WANTED
DEAD OR ALIVE
VINSMOKE SANJI
330,000,000-
MARINE
WANTED
DEAD OR ALIVE
NICO ROBIN
130,000,000-
MARINE

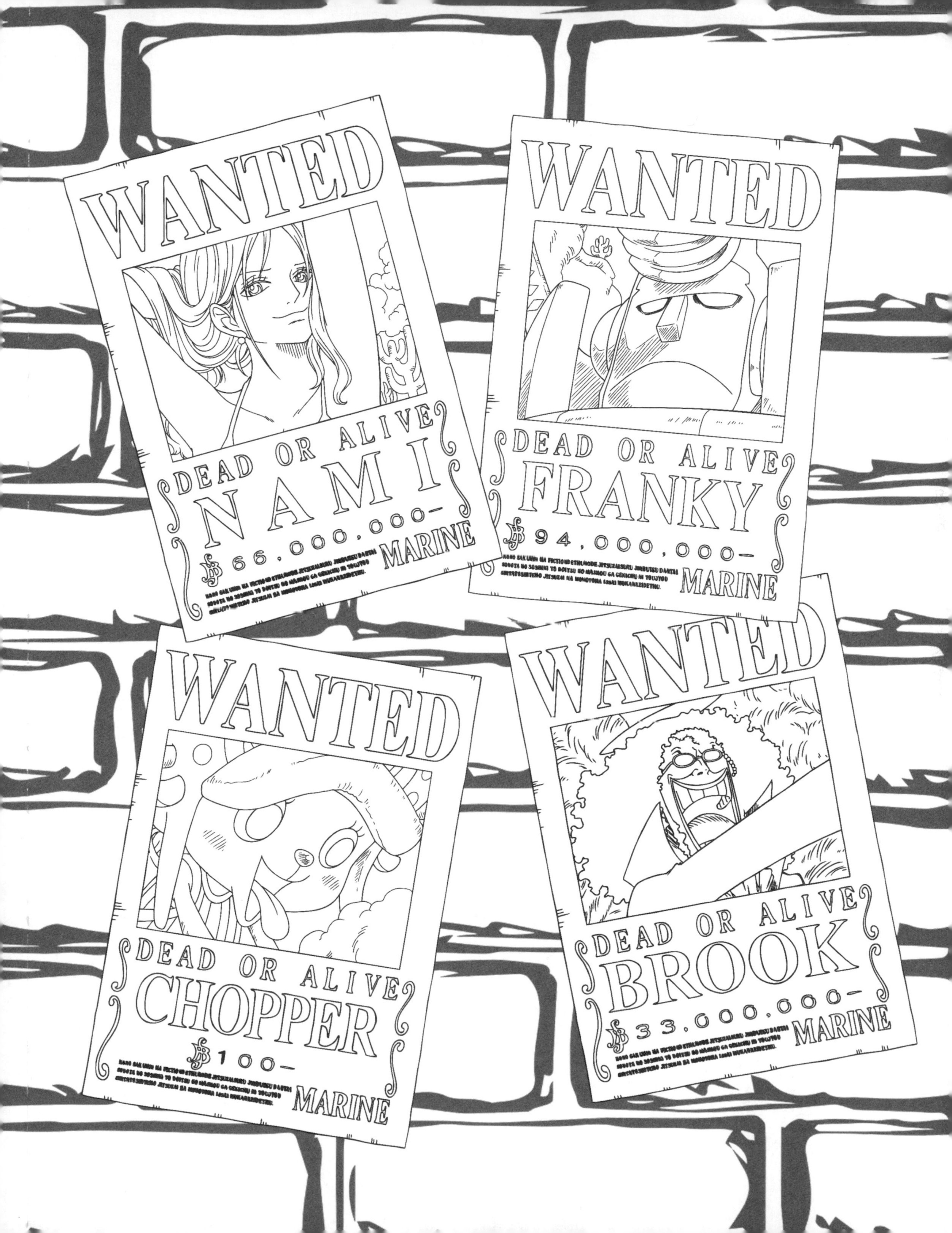
WANTED
DEAD OR ALIVE
NAMI
฿66,000,000-
MARINE
WANTED
DEAD OR ALIVE
FRANKY
฿94,000,000-
MARINE
WANTED
DEAD OR ALIVE
CHOPPER
฿100-
MARINE
WANTED
DEAD OR ALIVE
BROOK
฿33,000,000-
MARINE

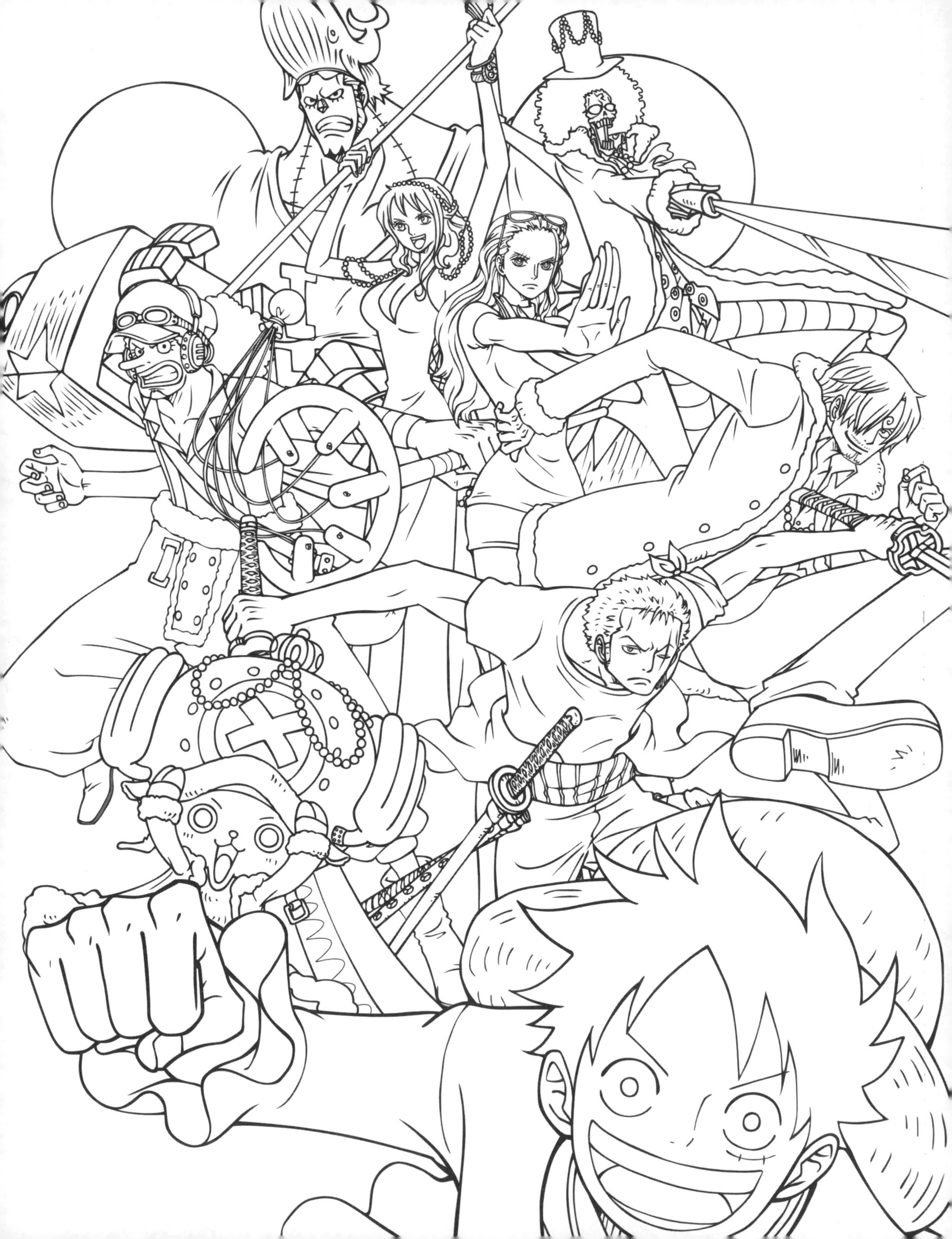

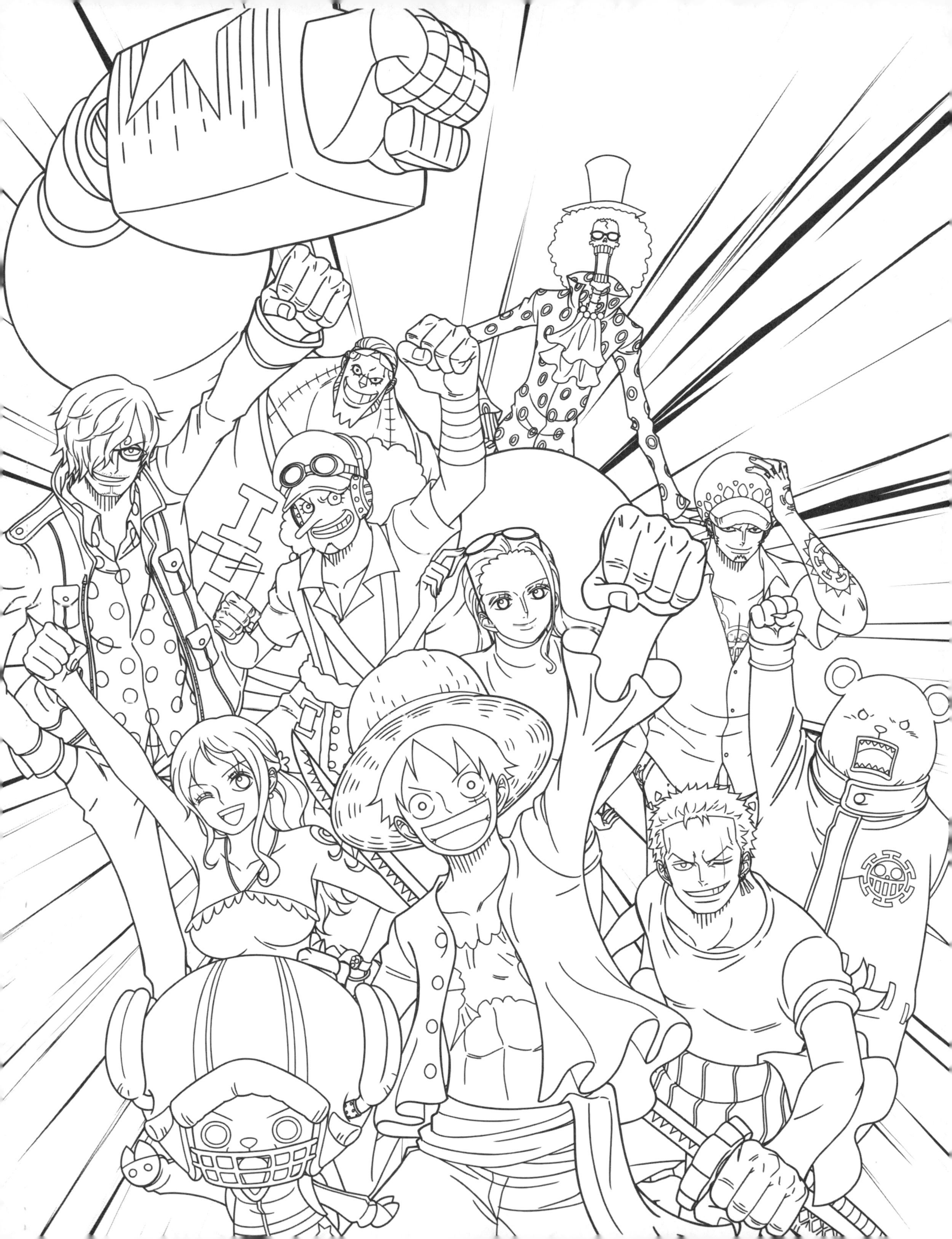

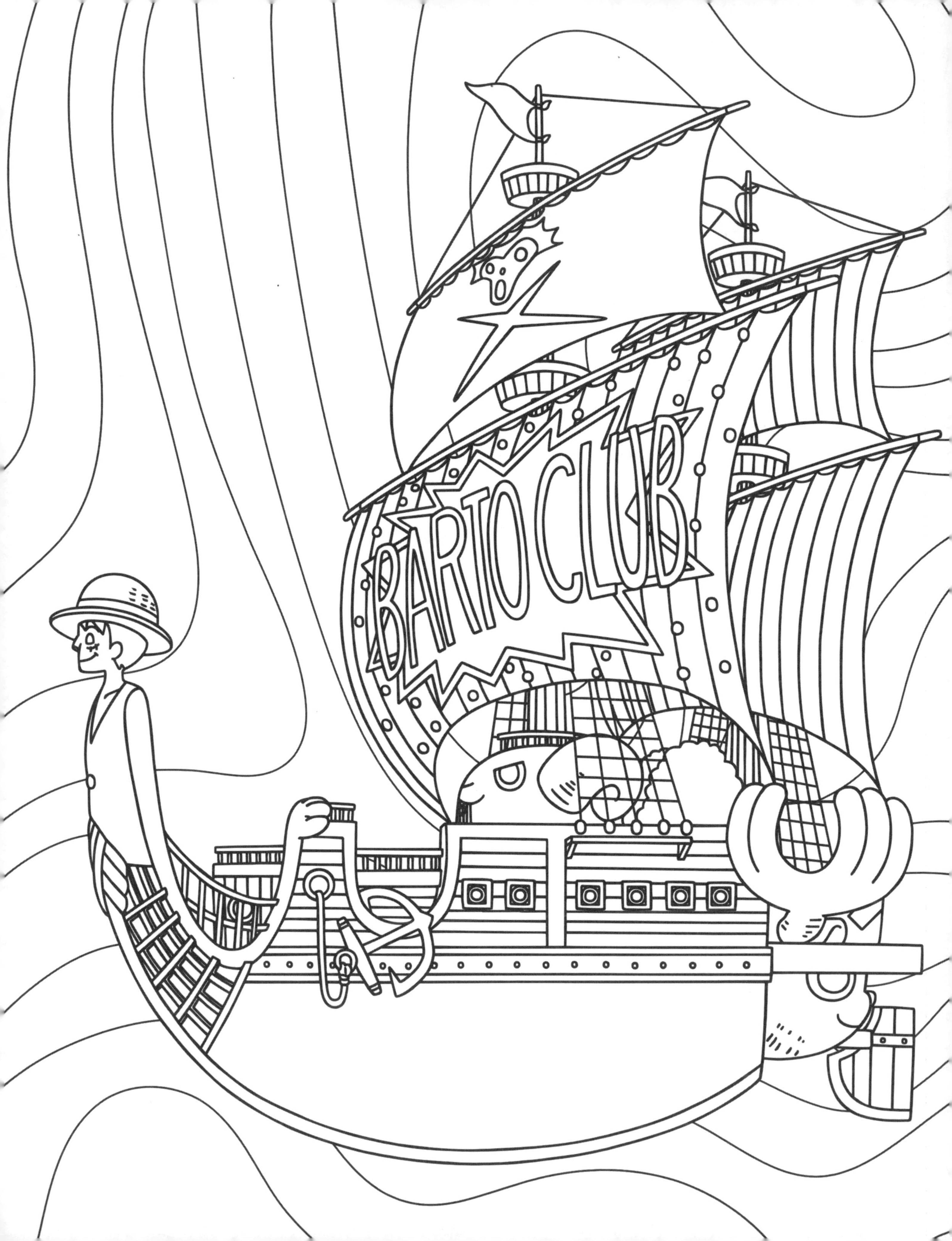
BARTO CLUB

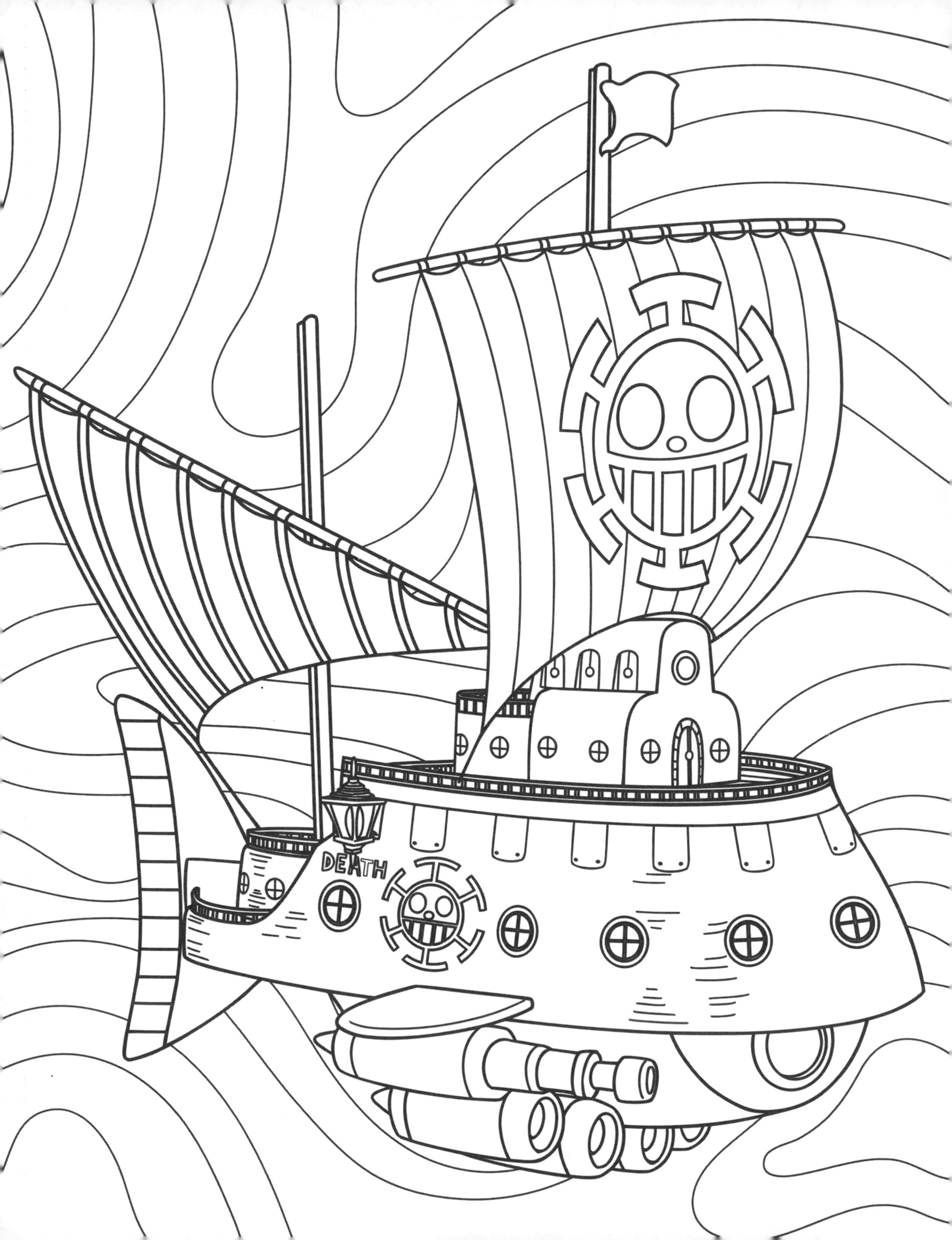
DEATH

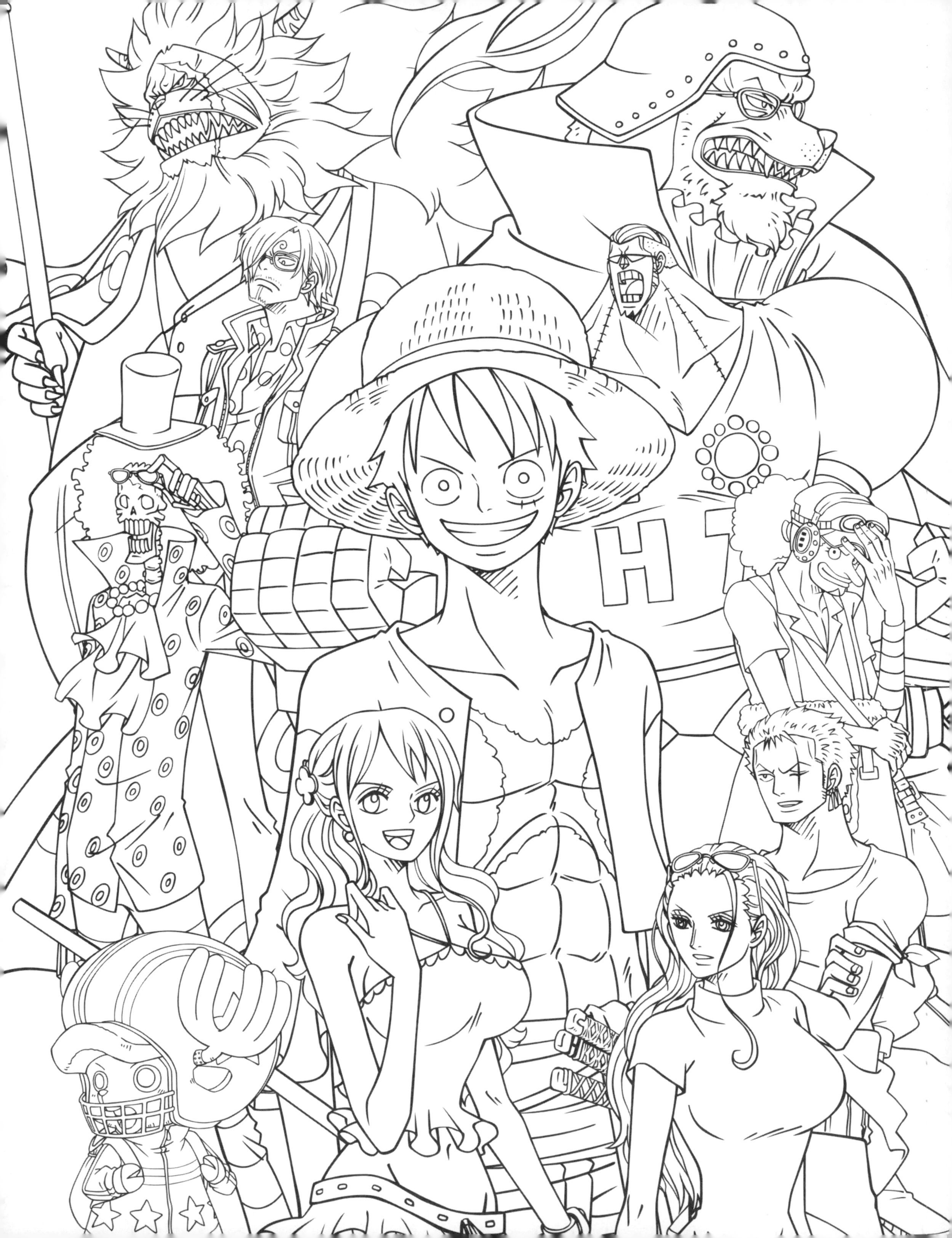

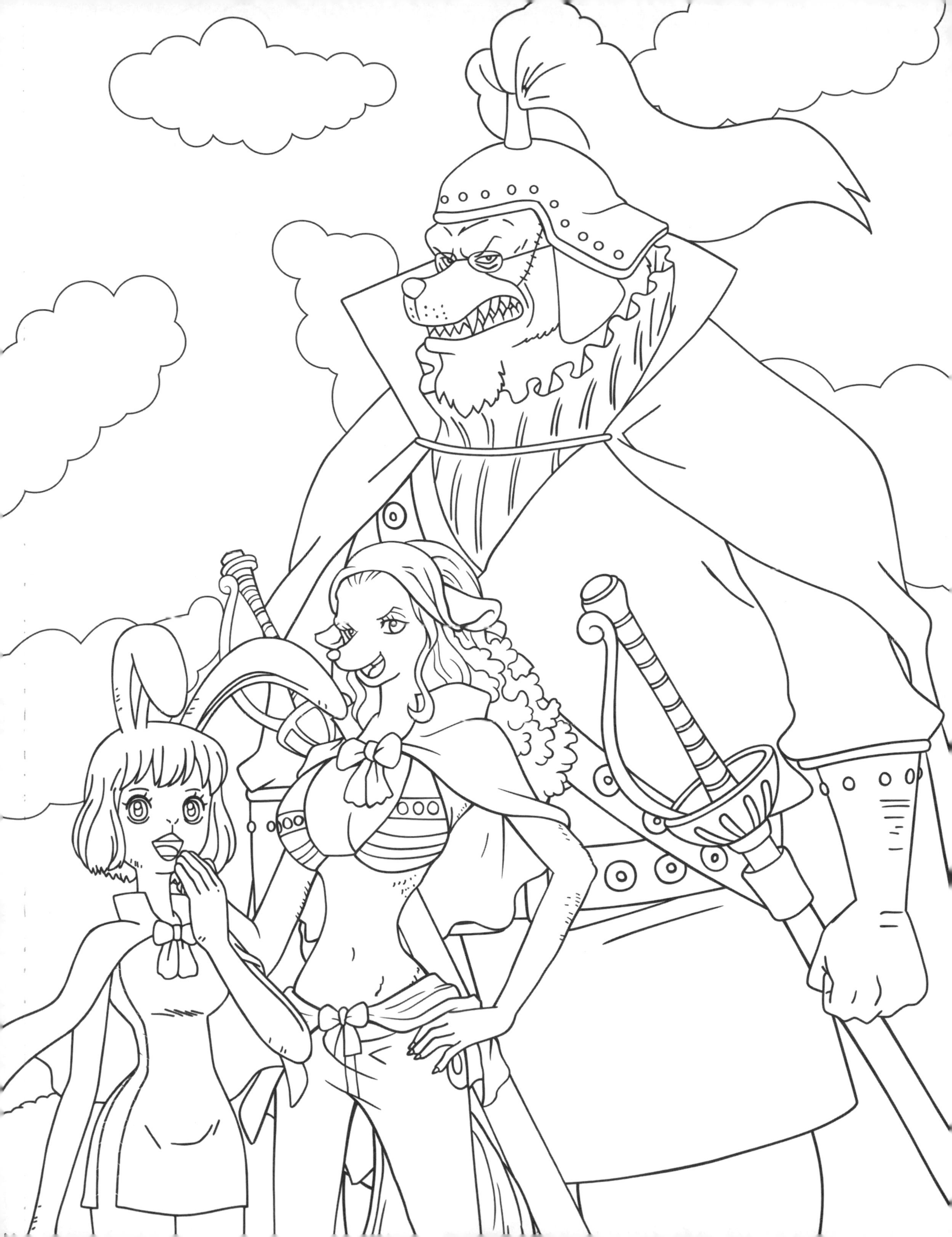

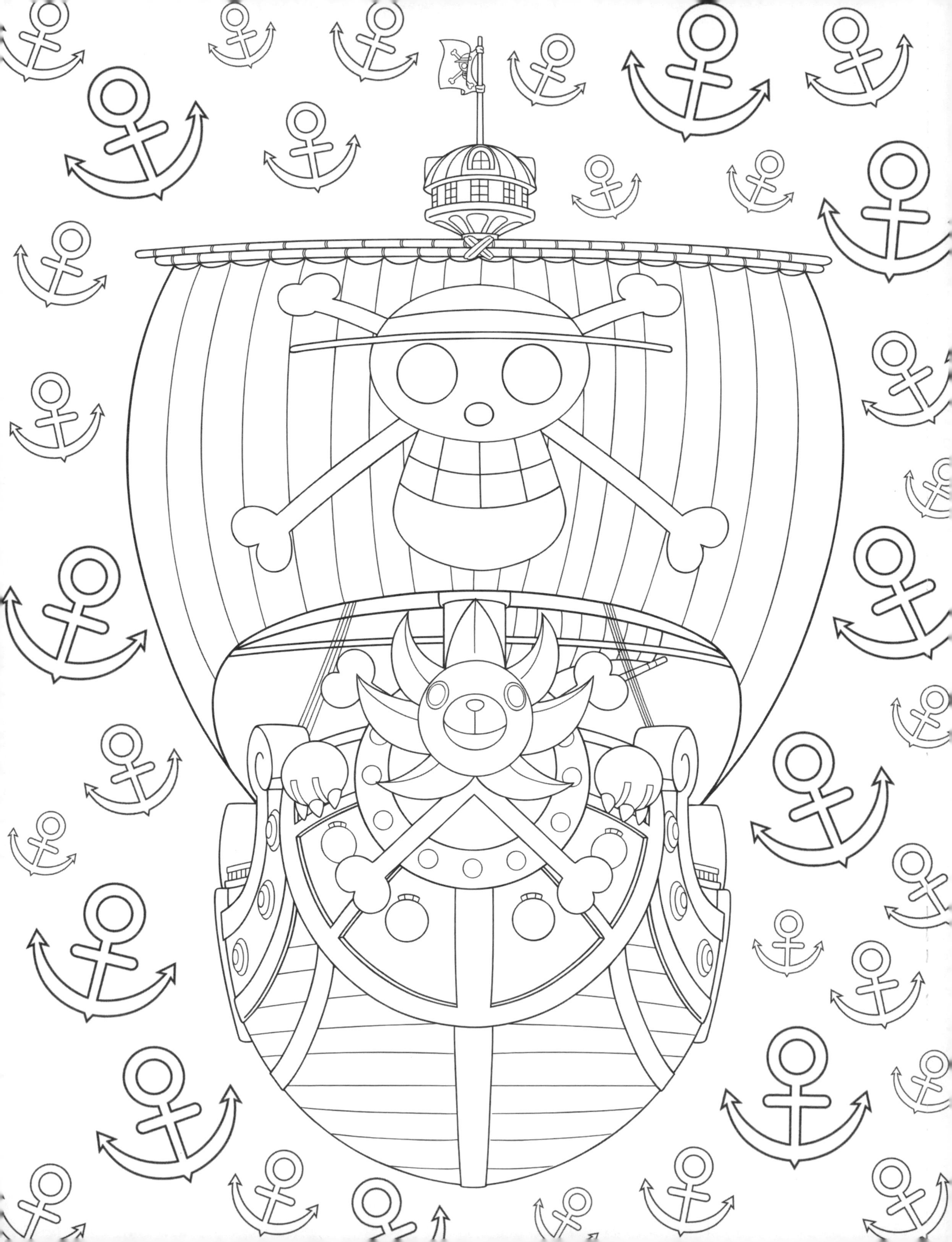

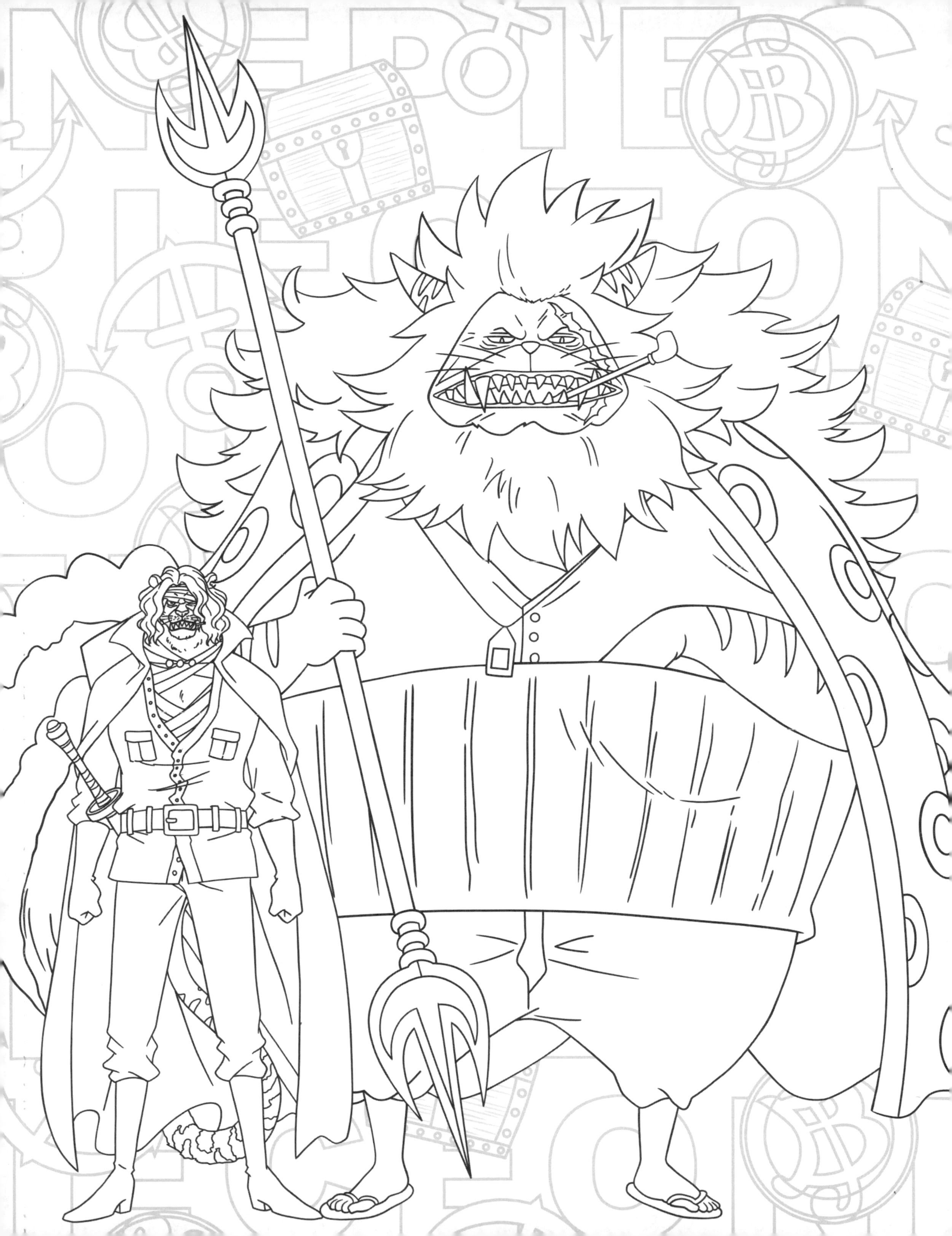

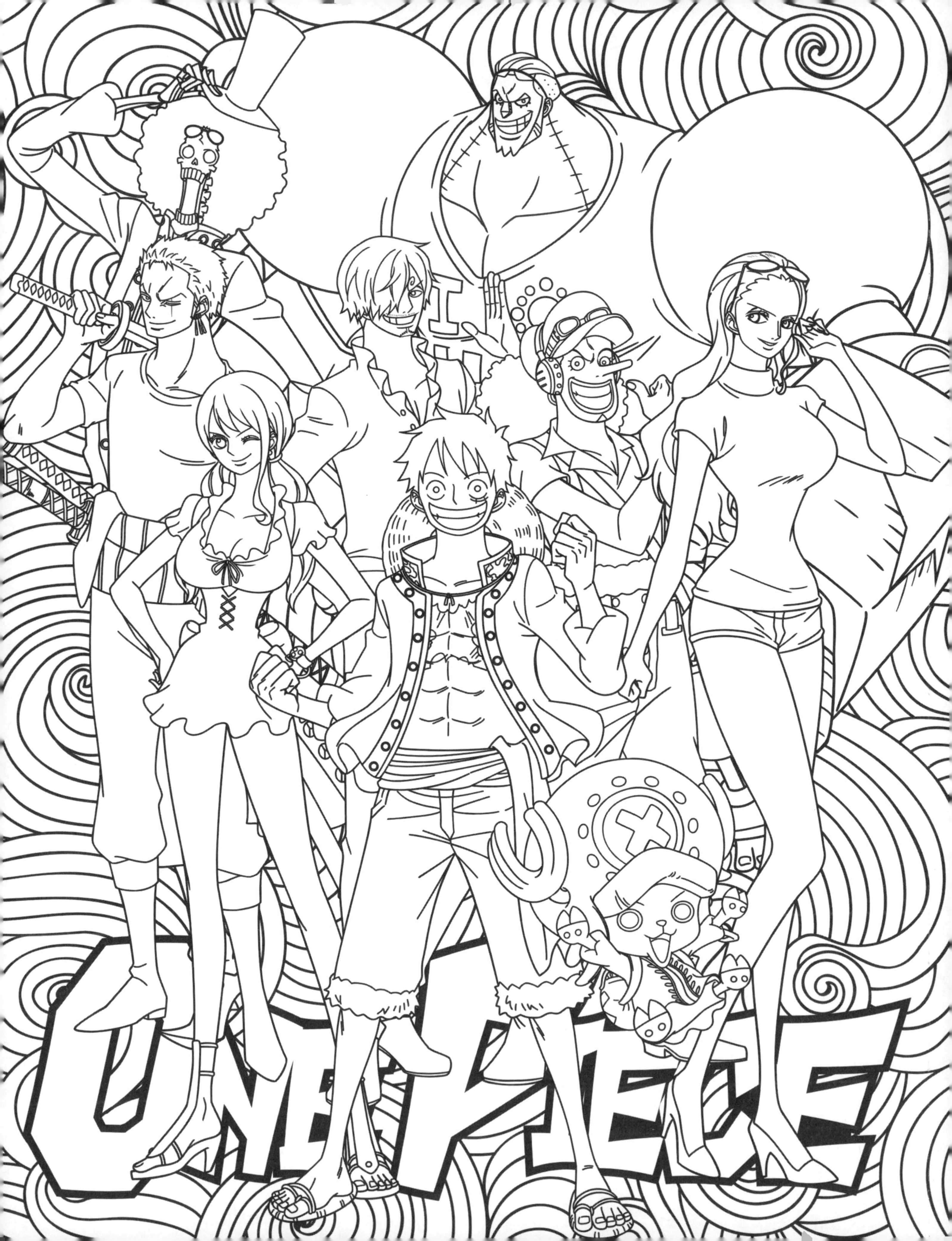

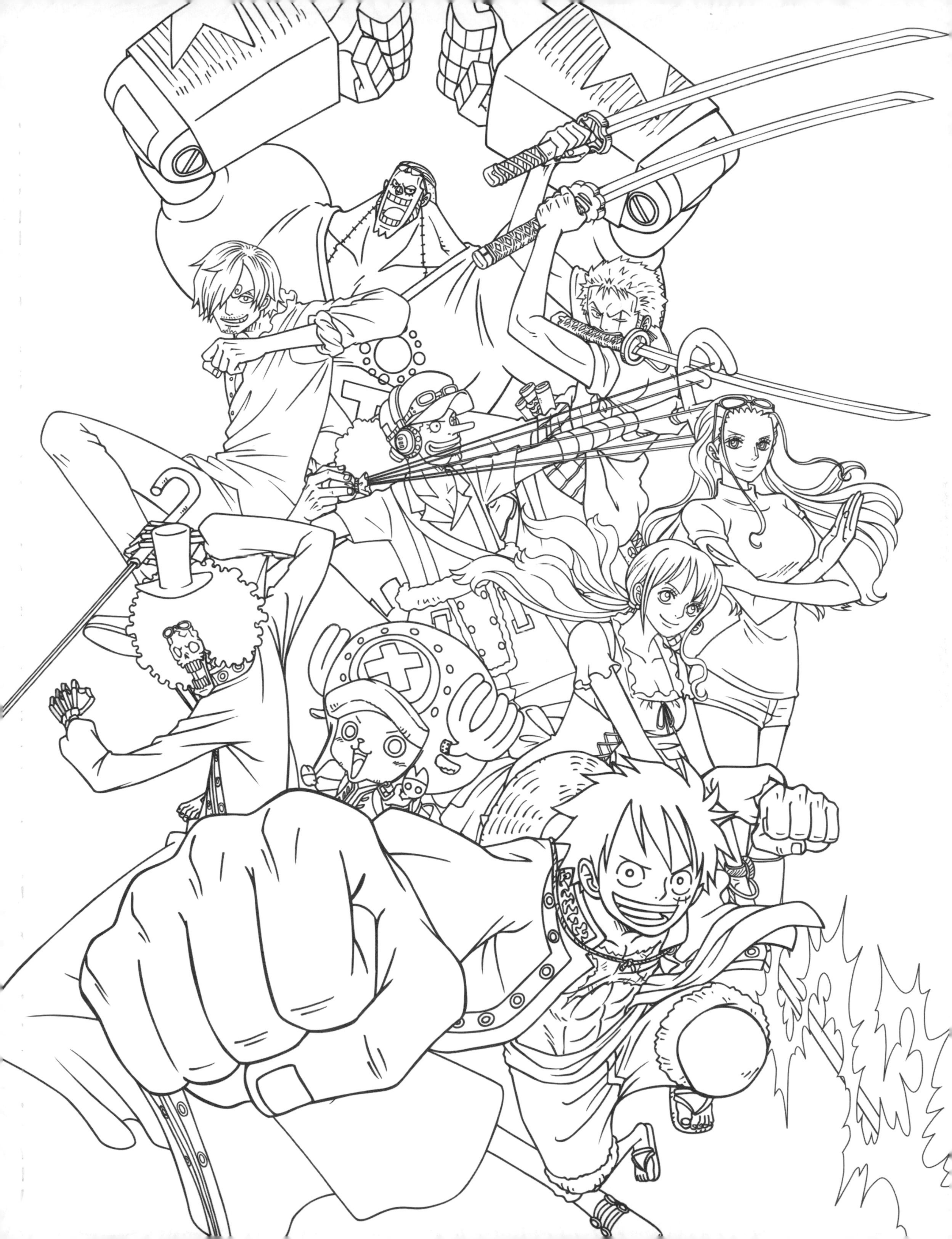

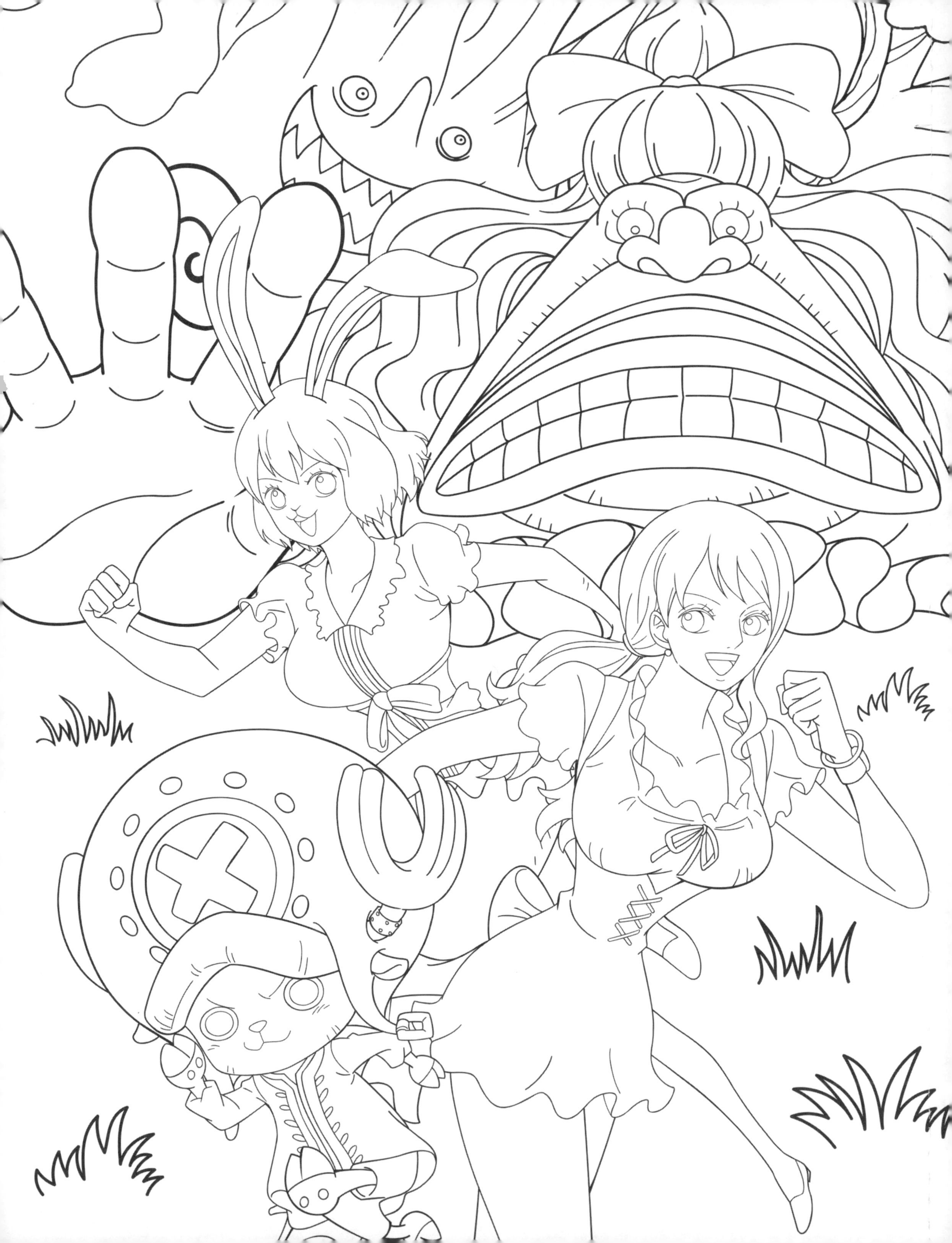

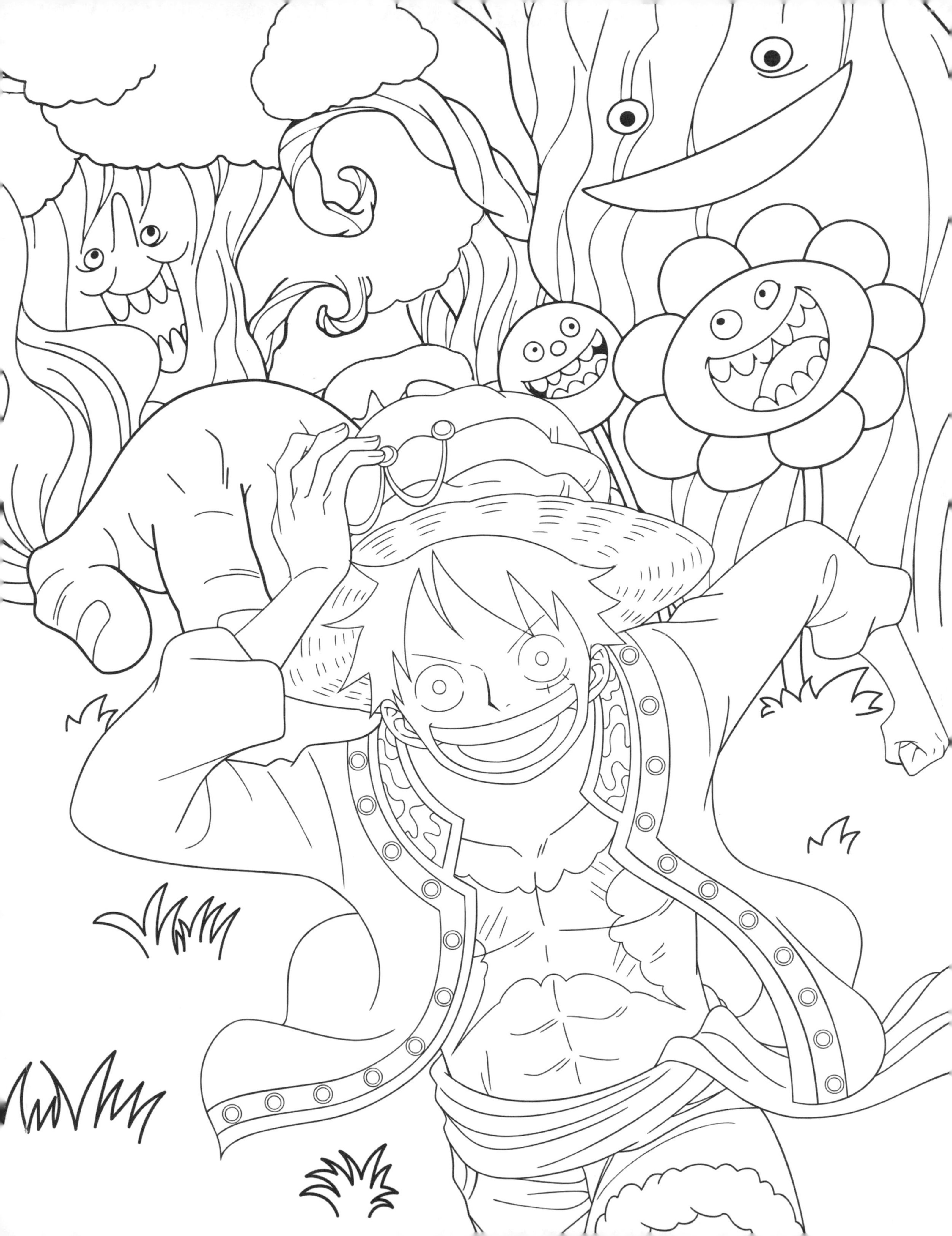

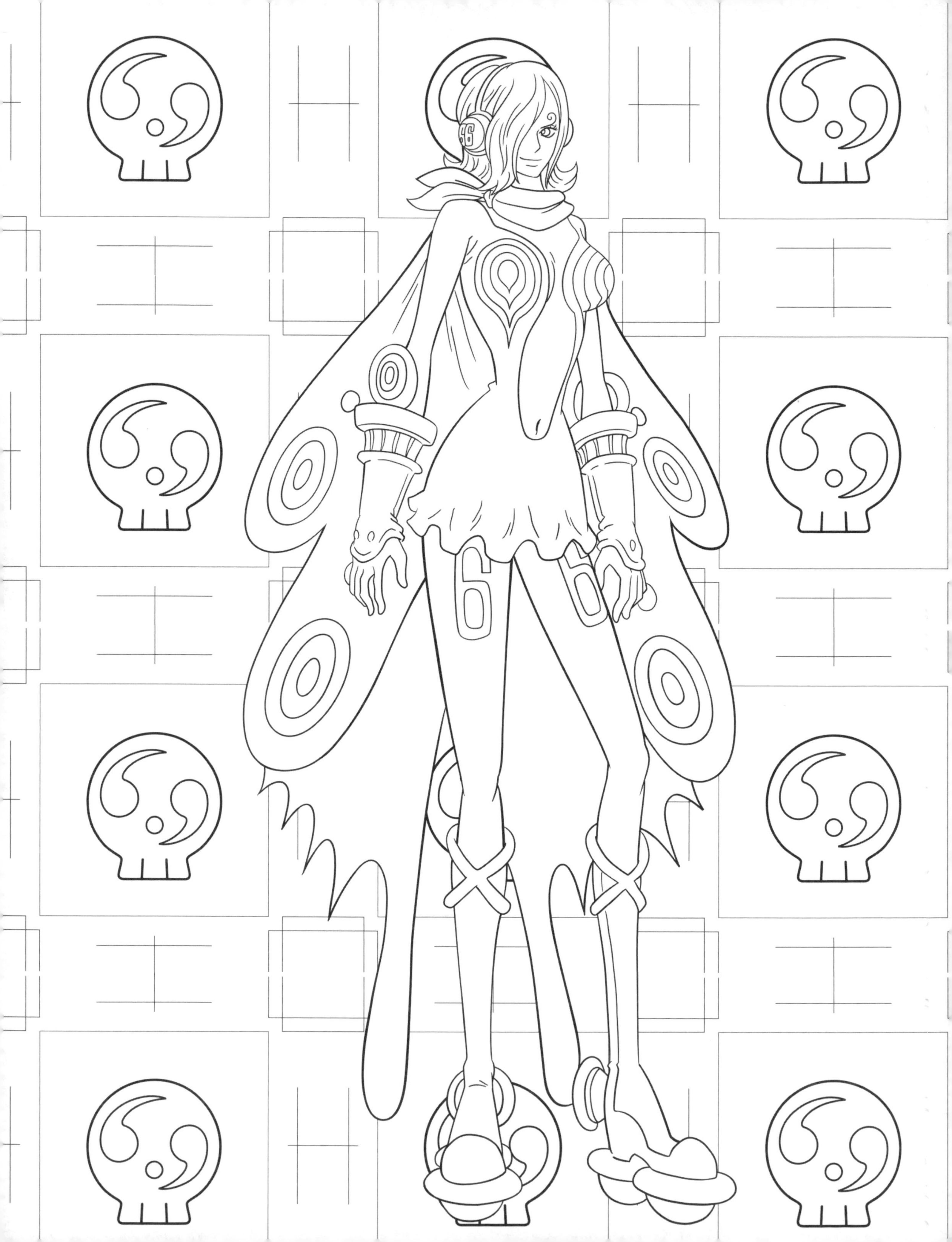

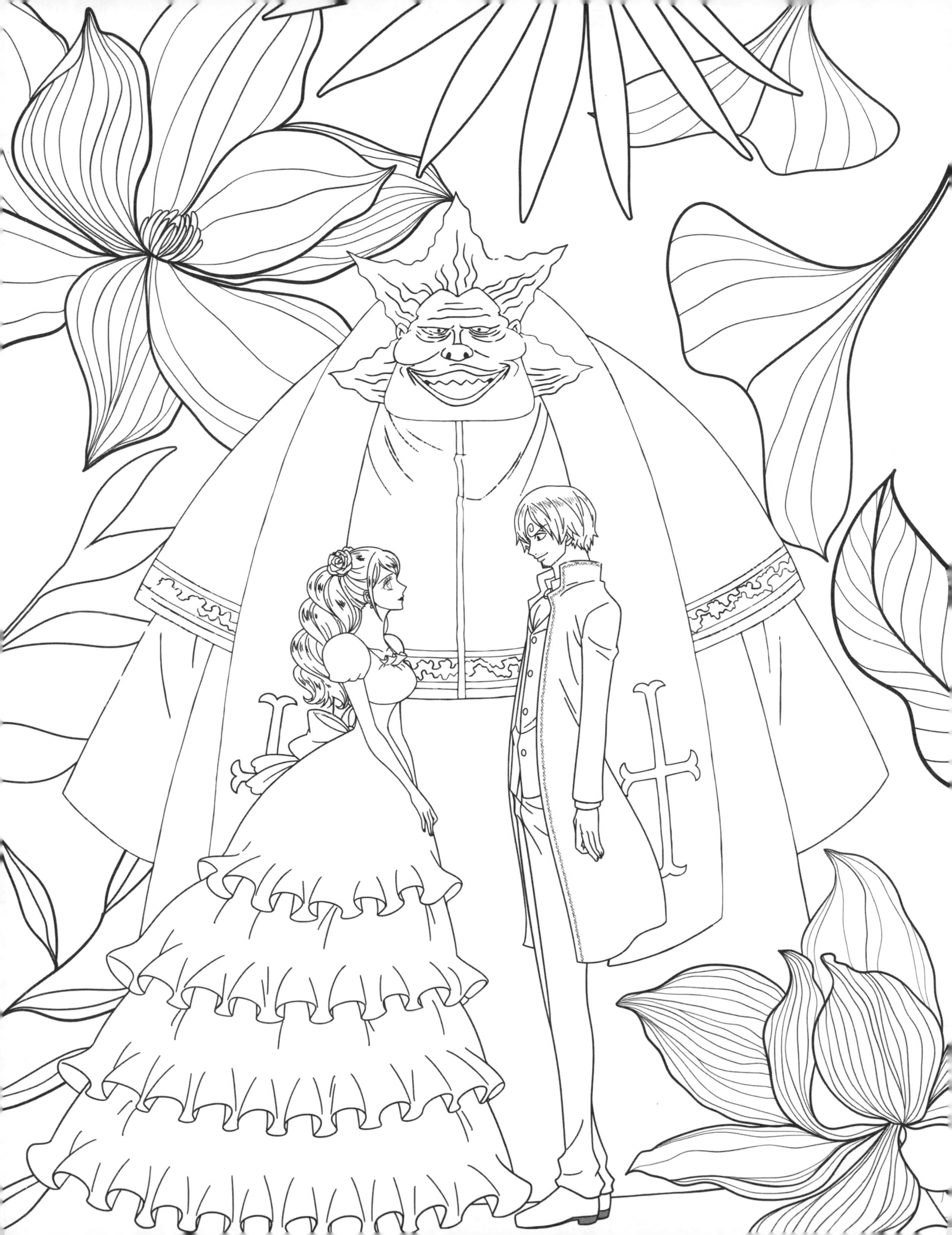

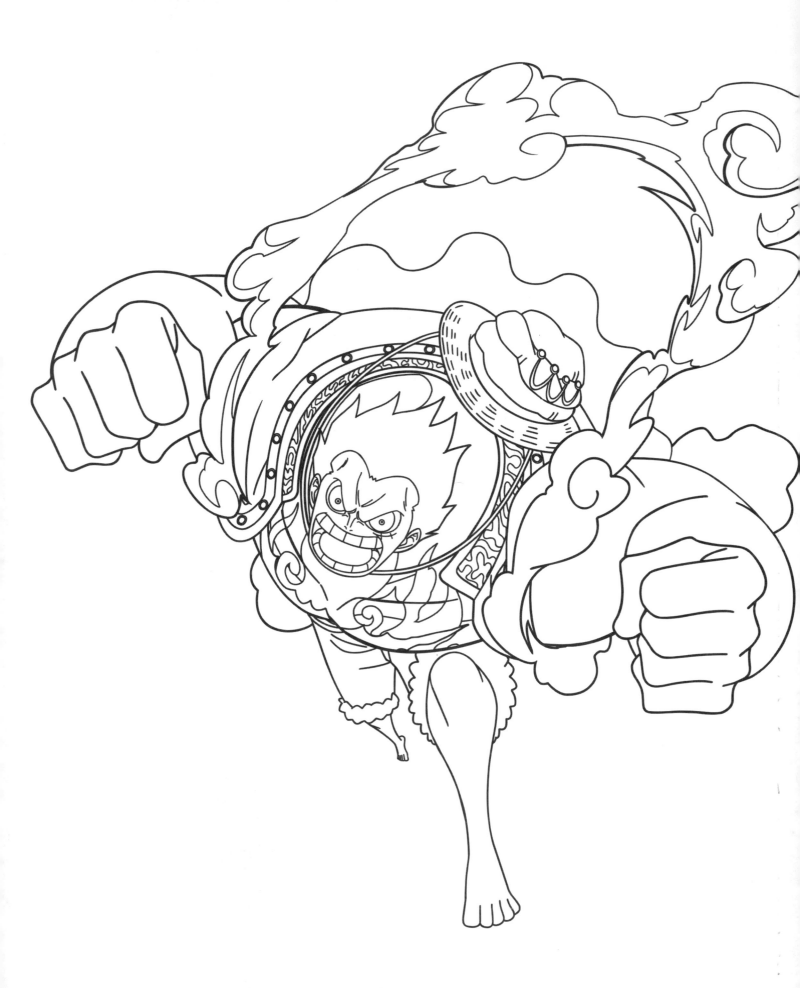

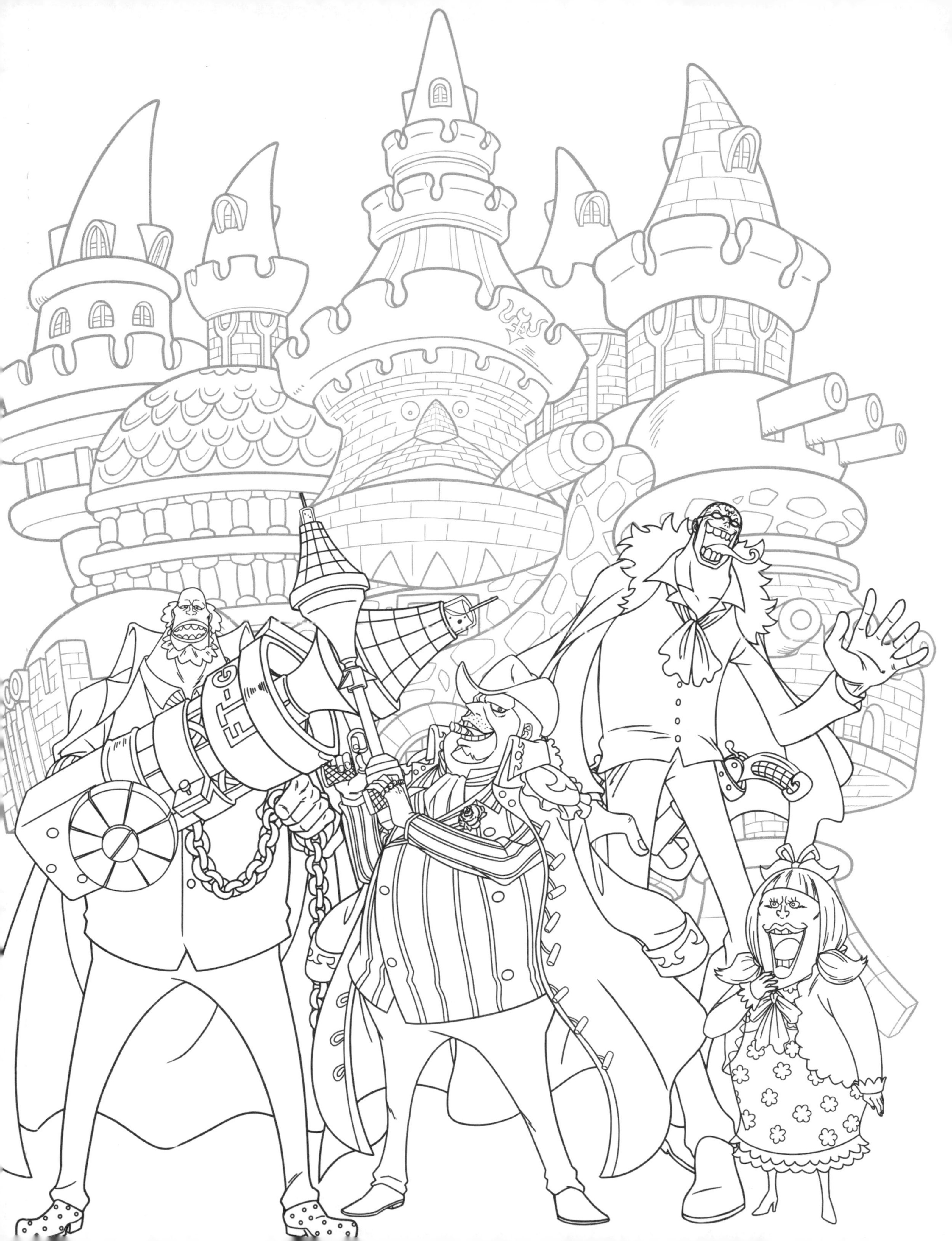

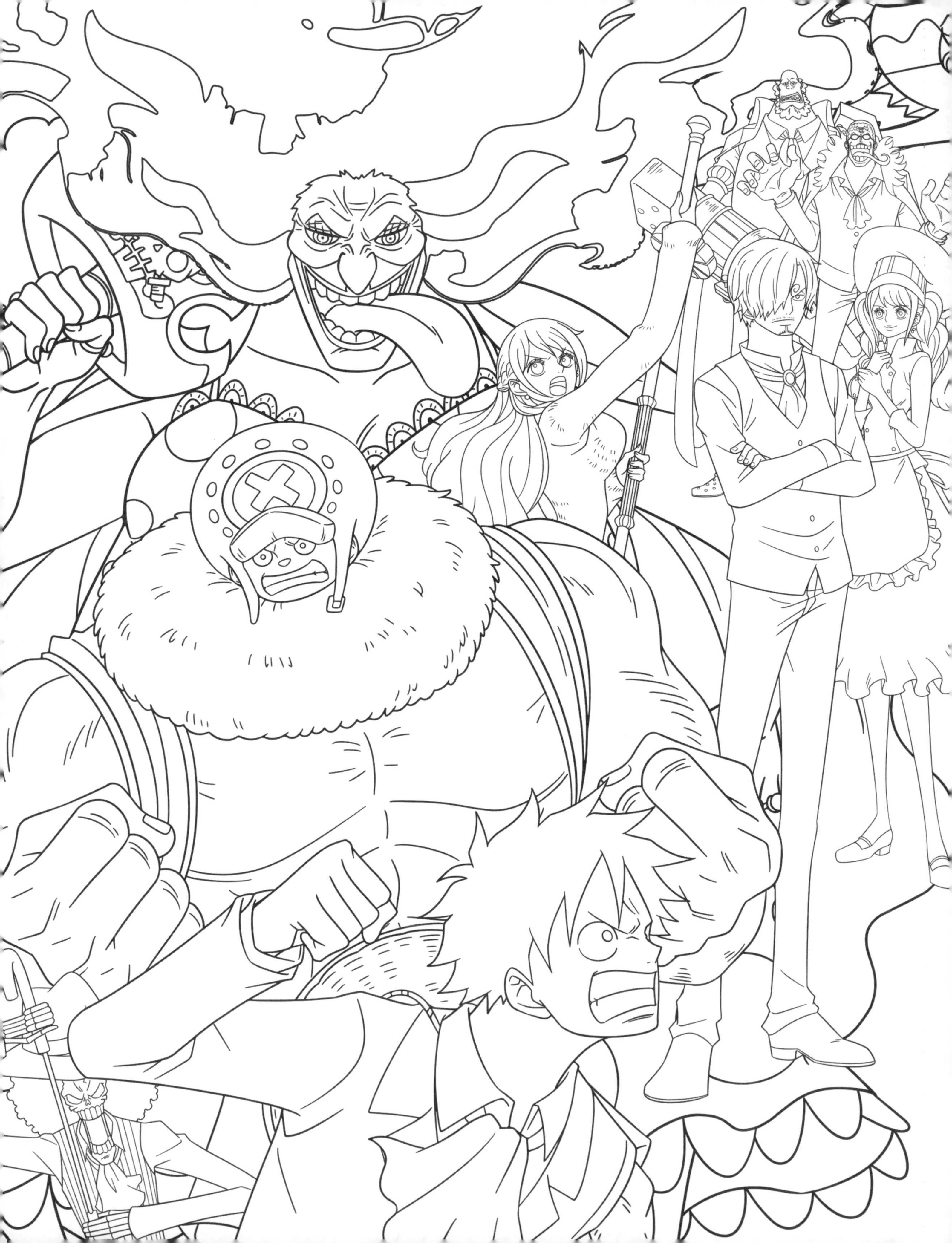

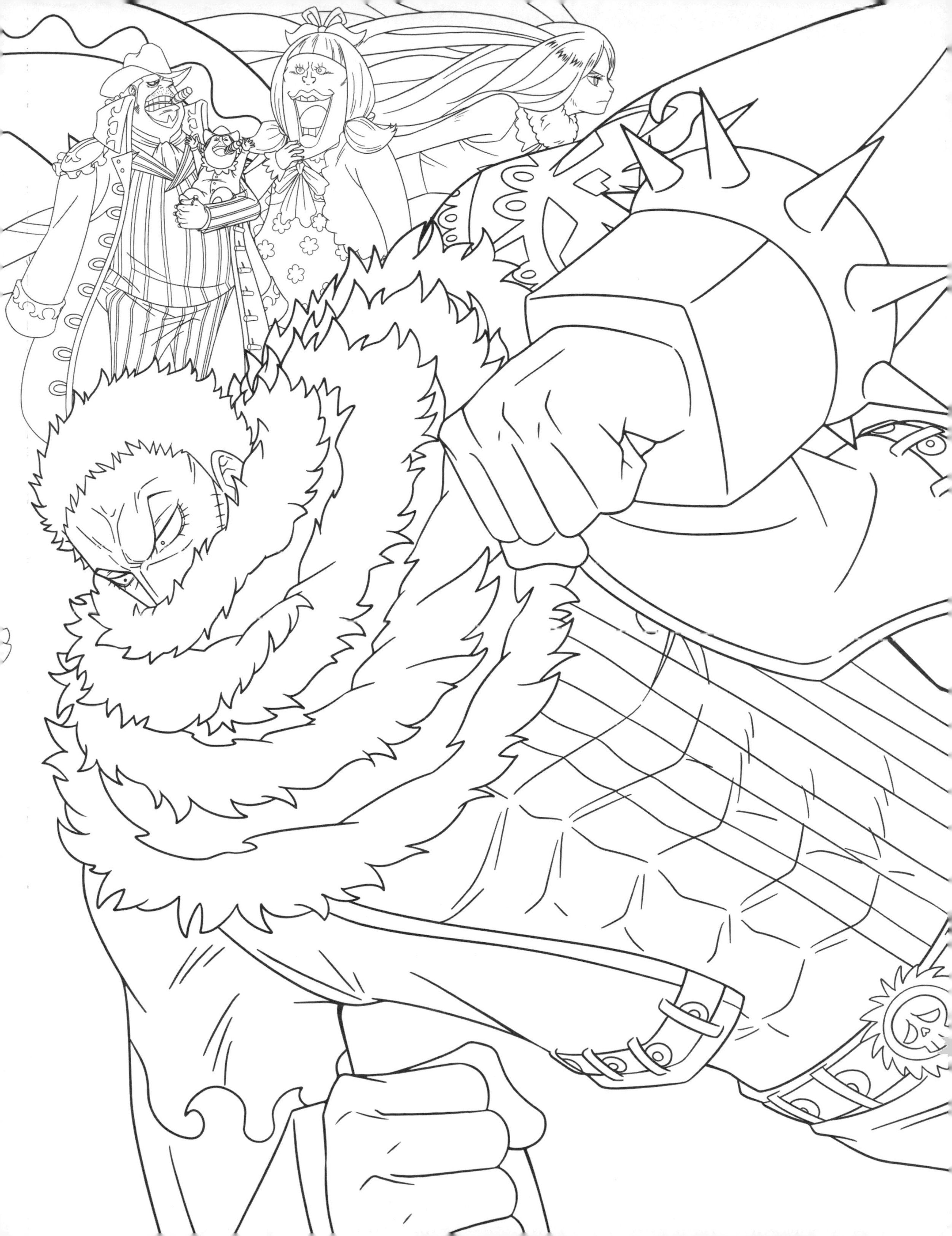

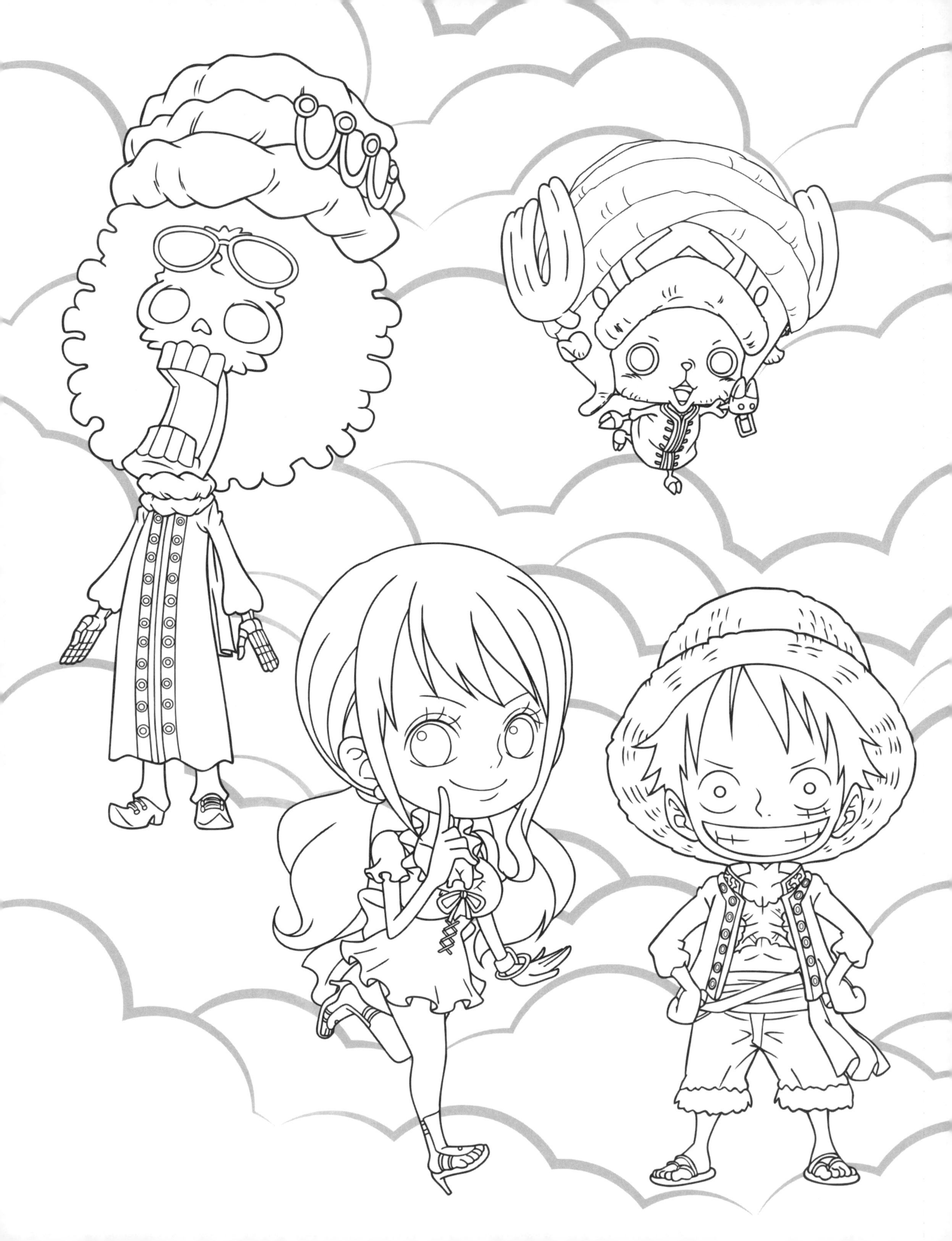

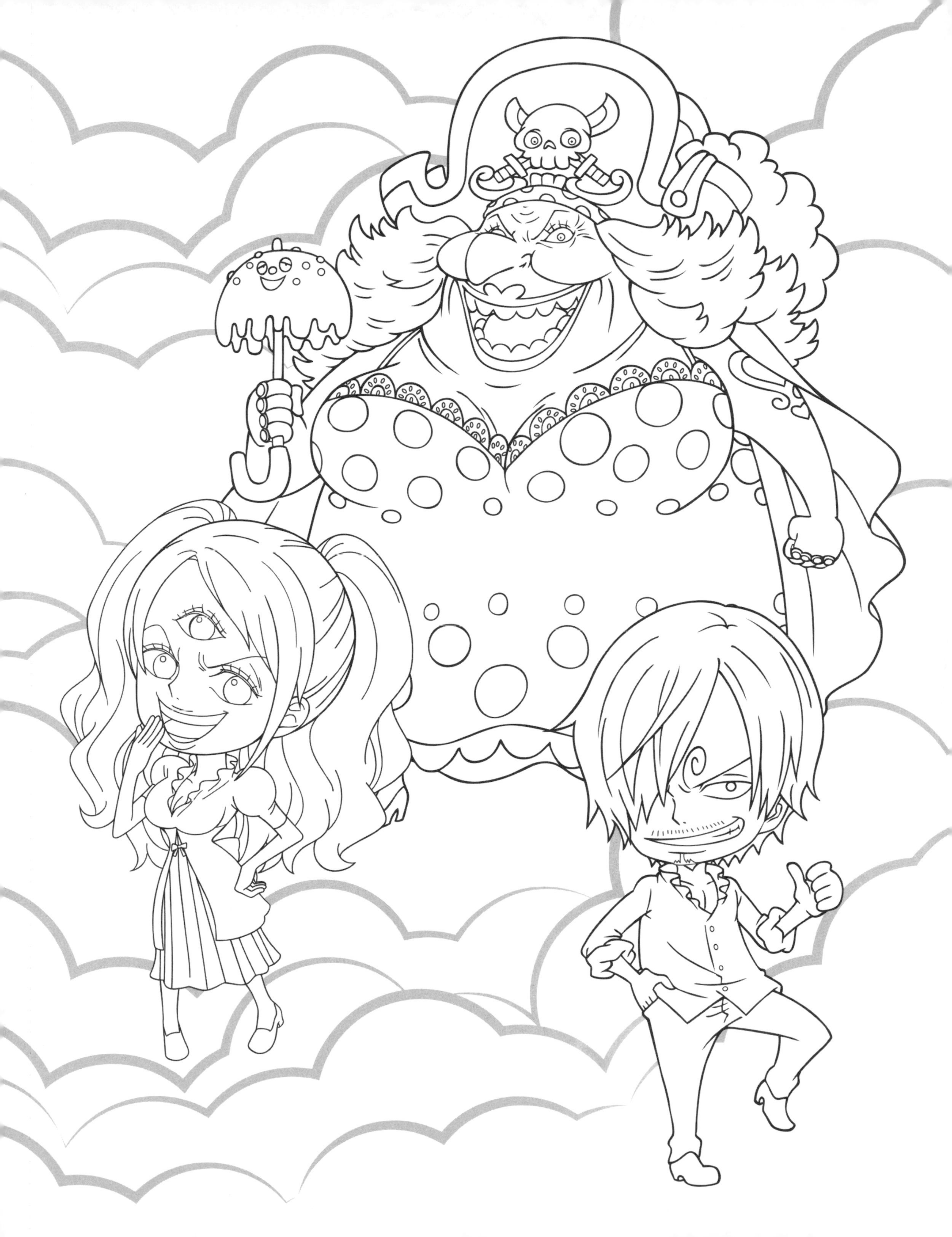

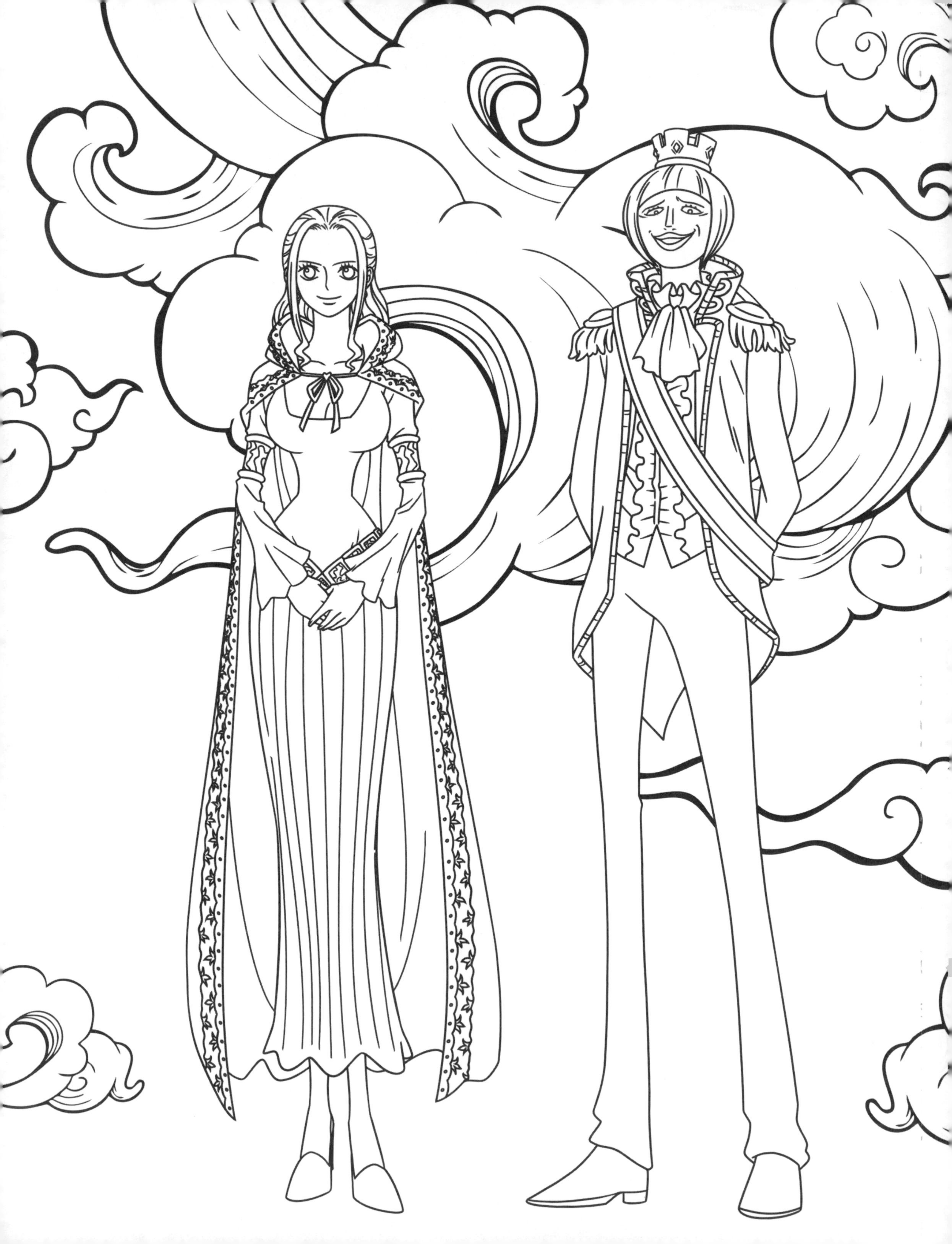

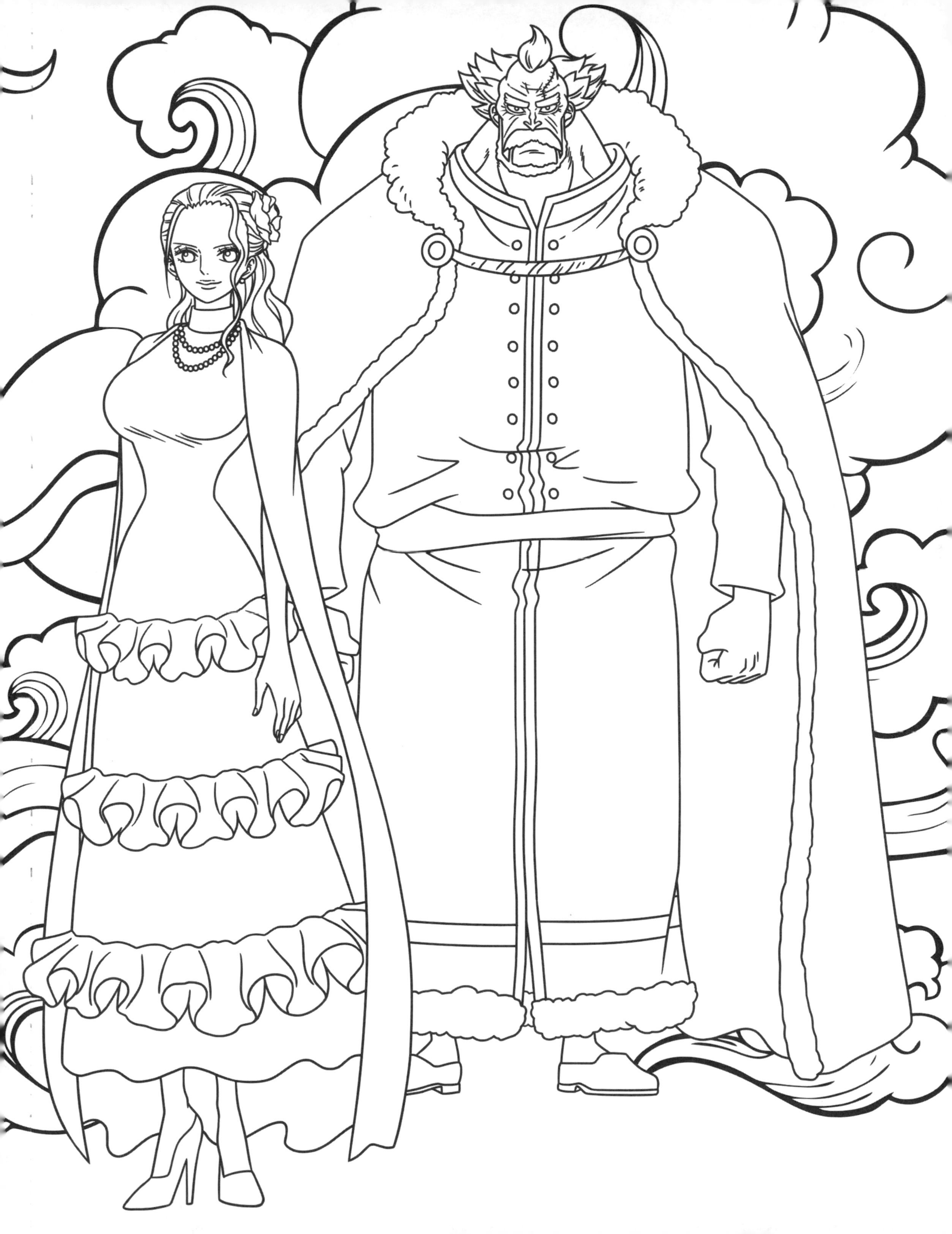

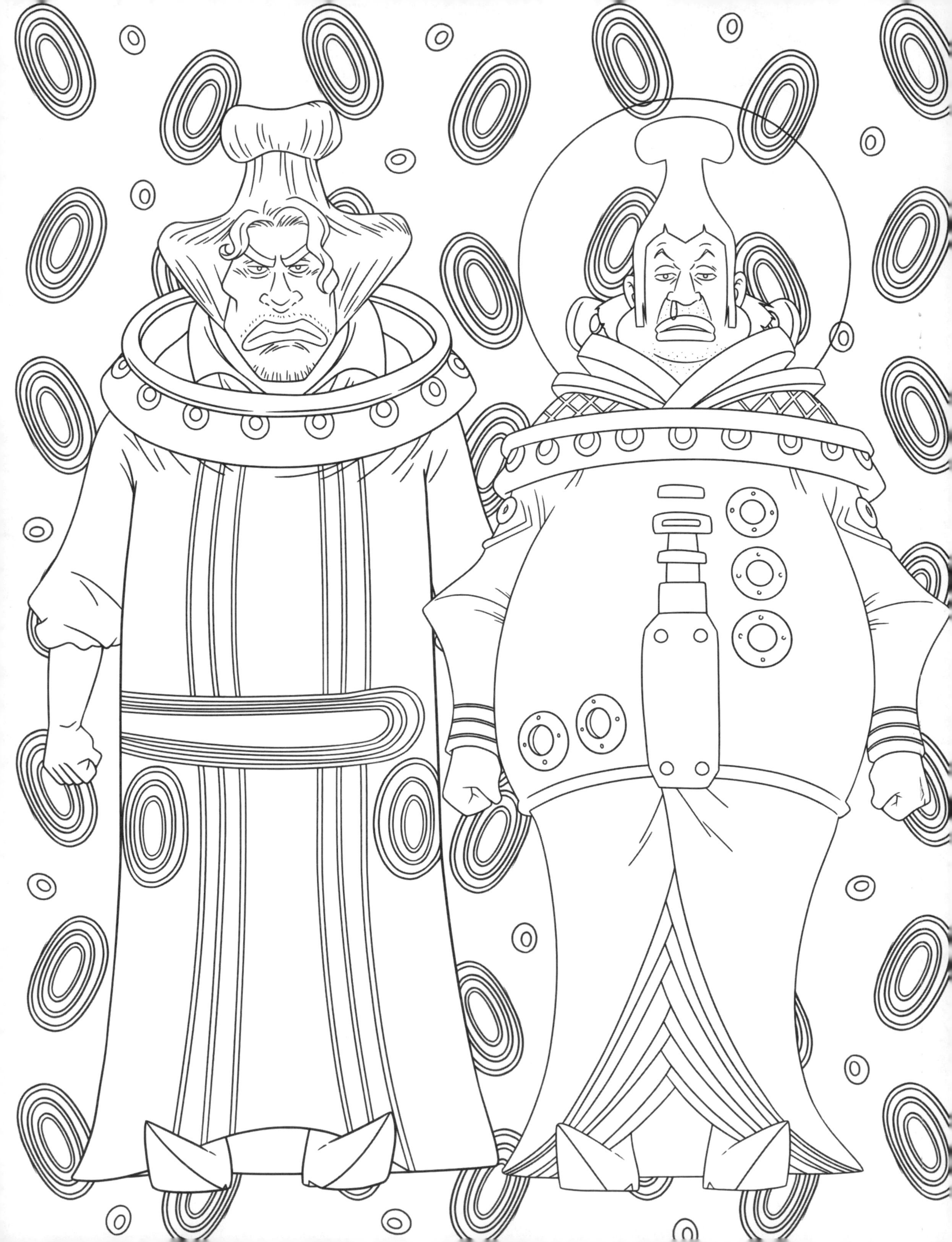

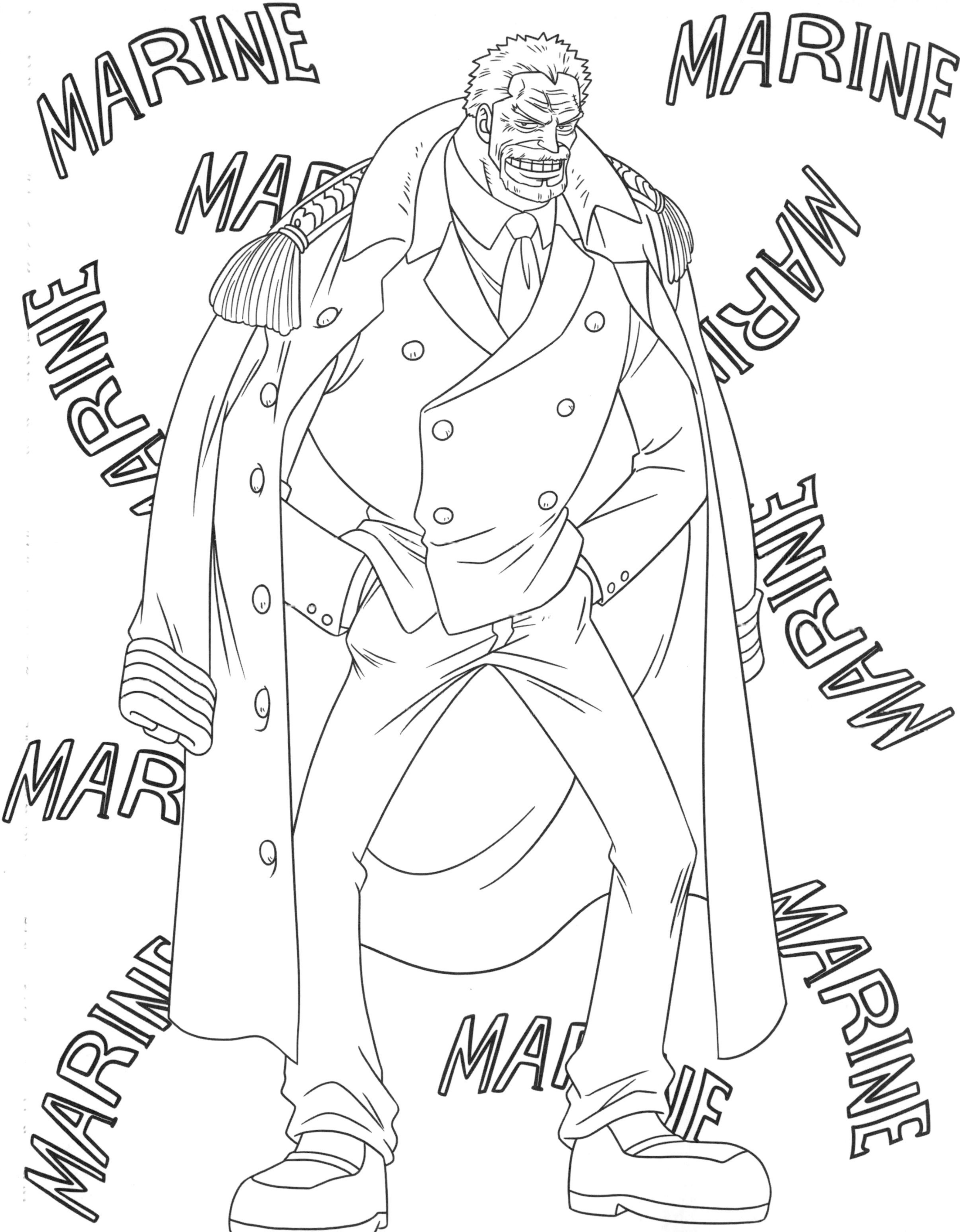
MARINE
MARINE
MARINE
MARINE
MARINE
MARINE
MARINE

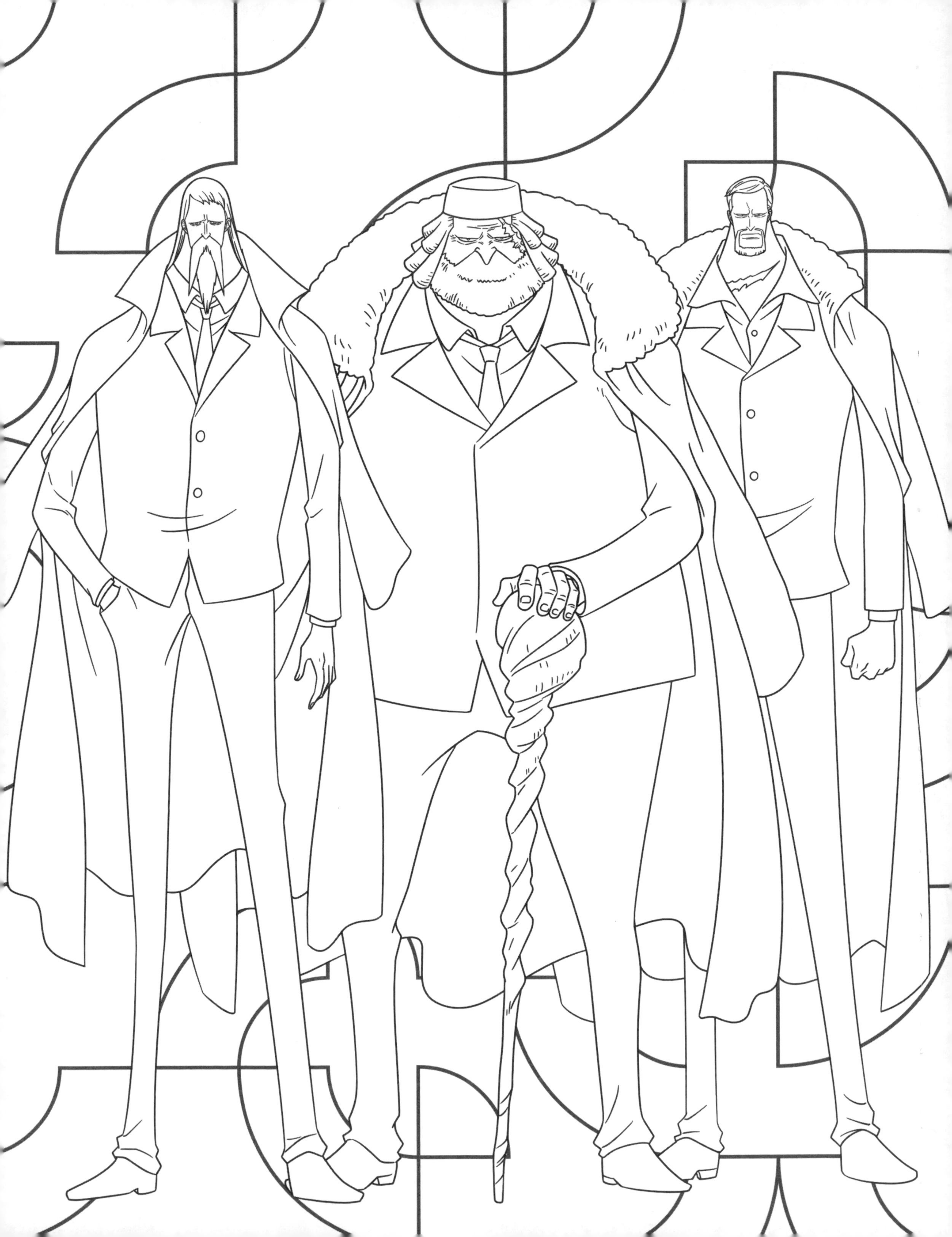

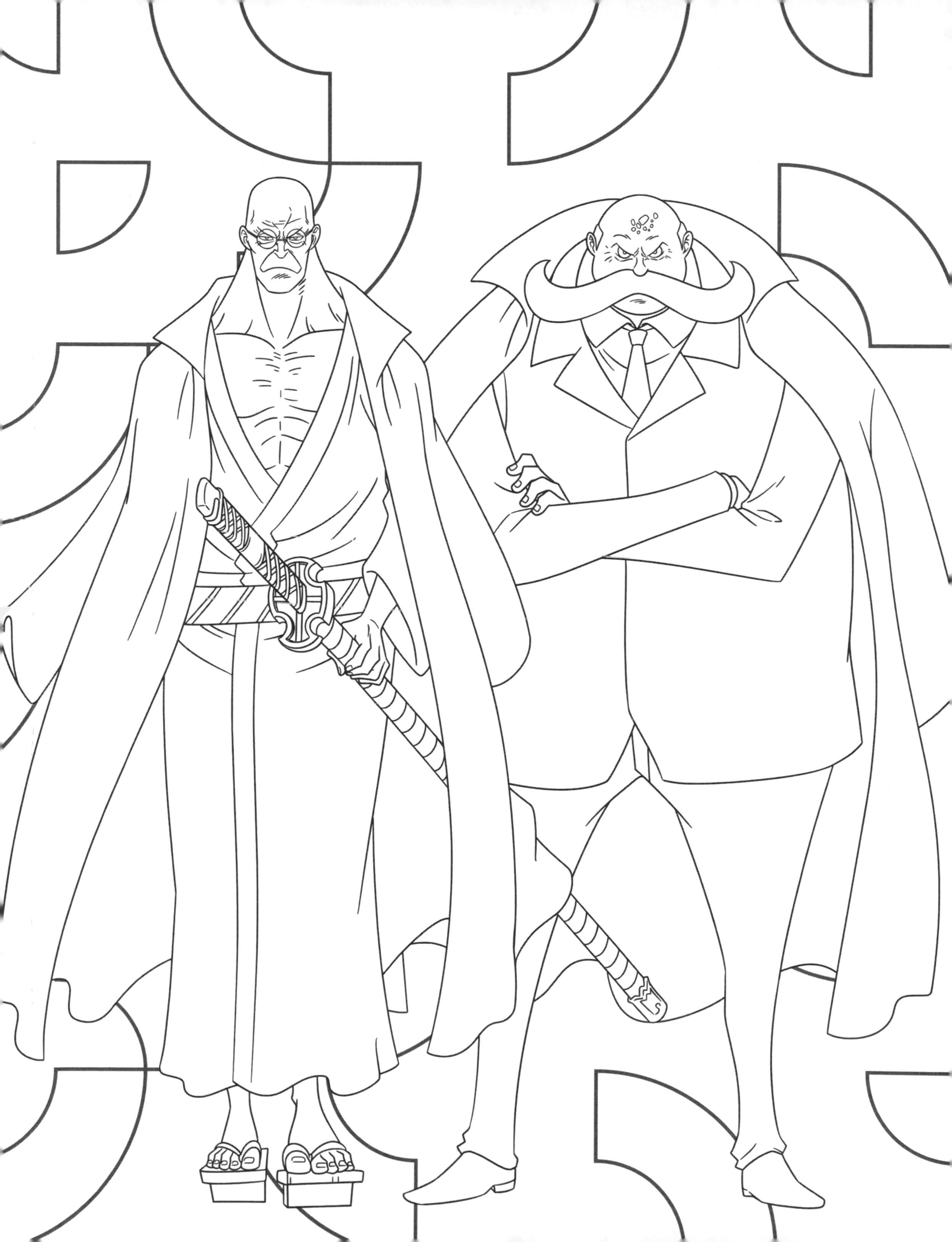

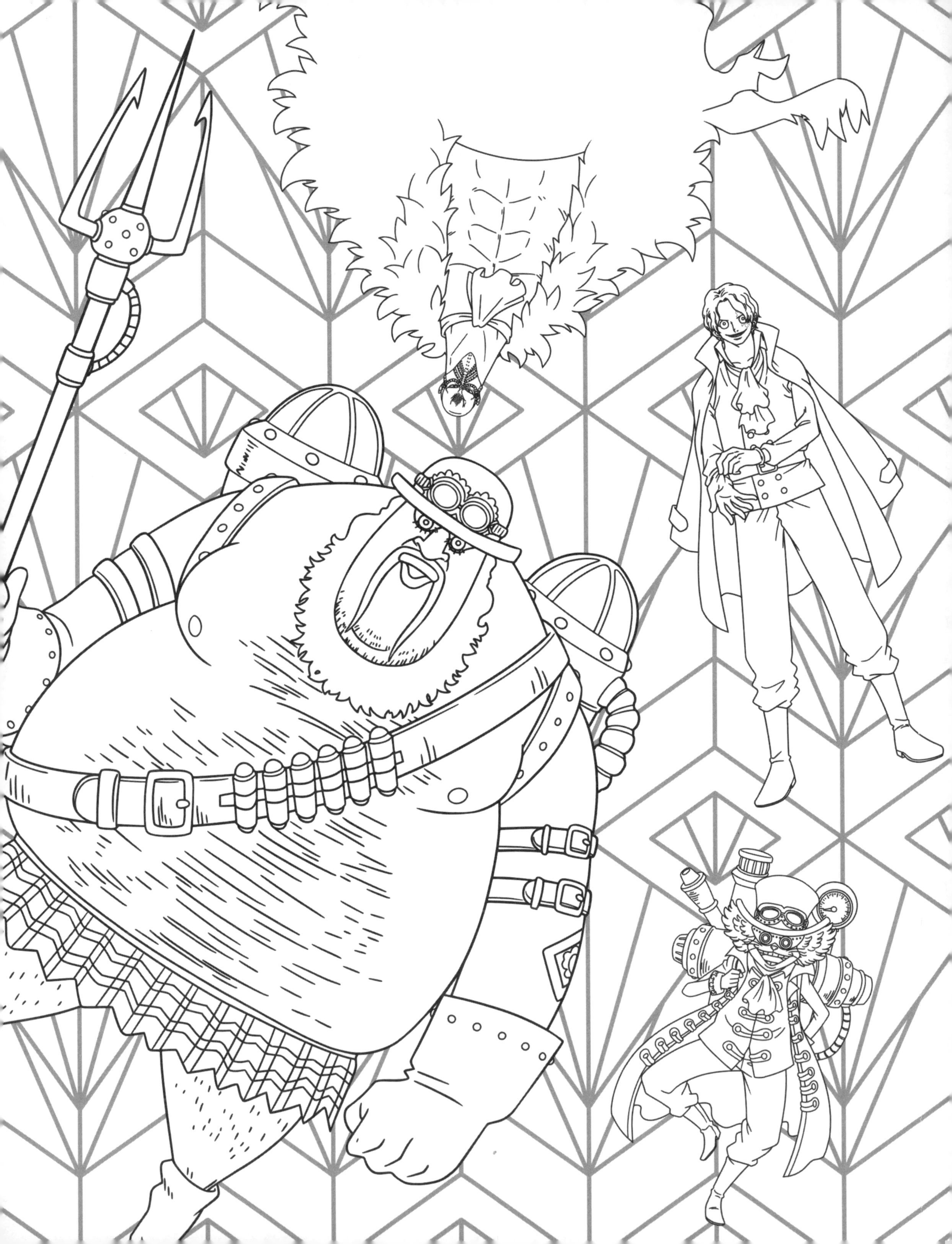

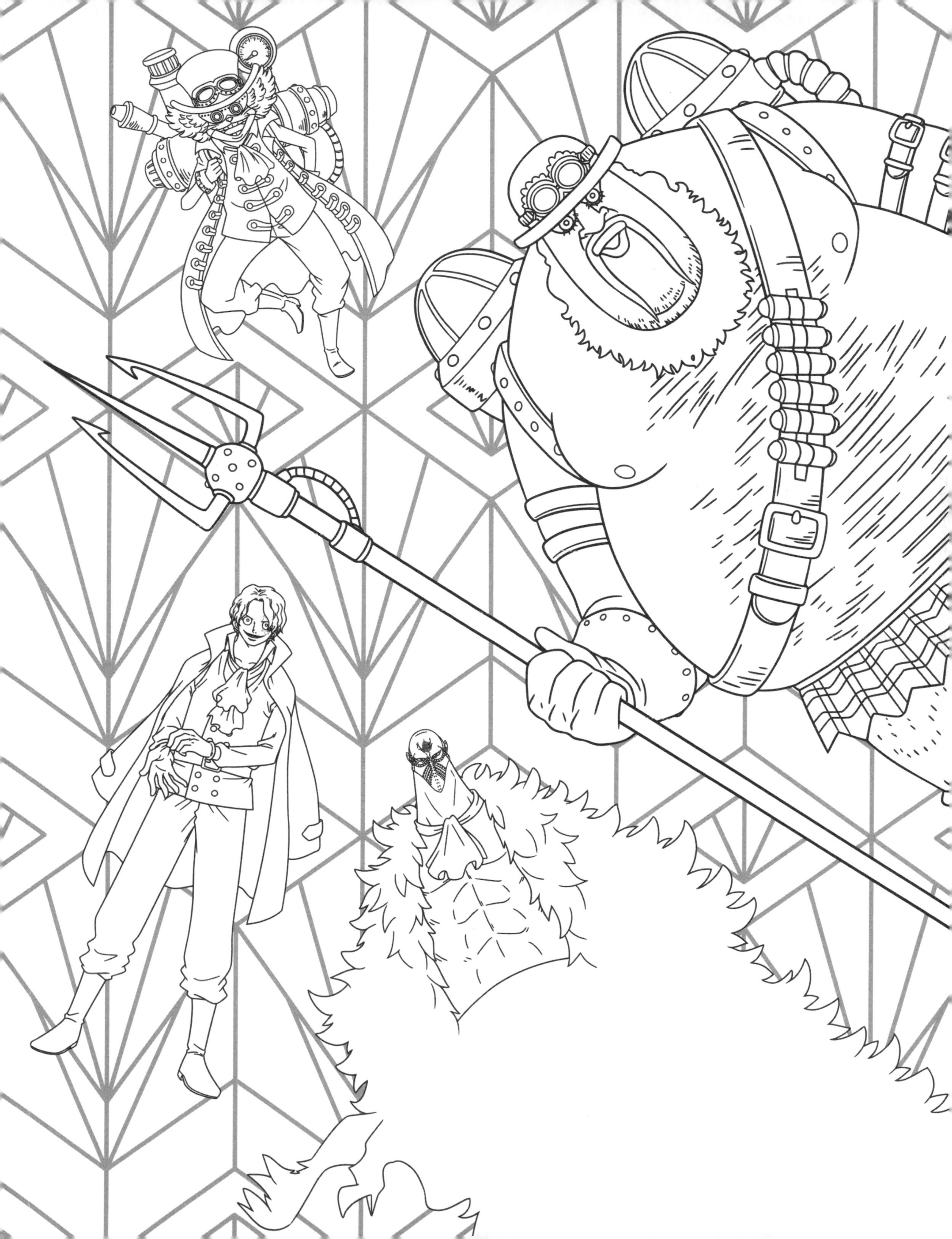

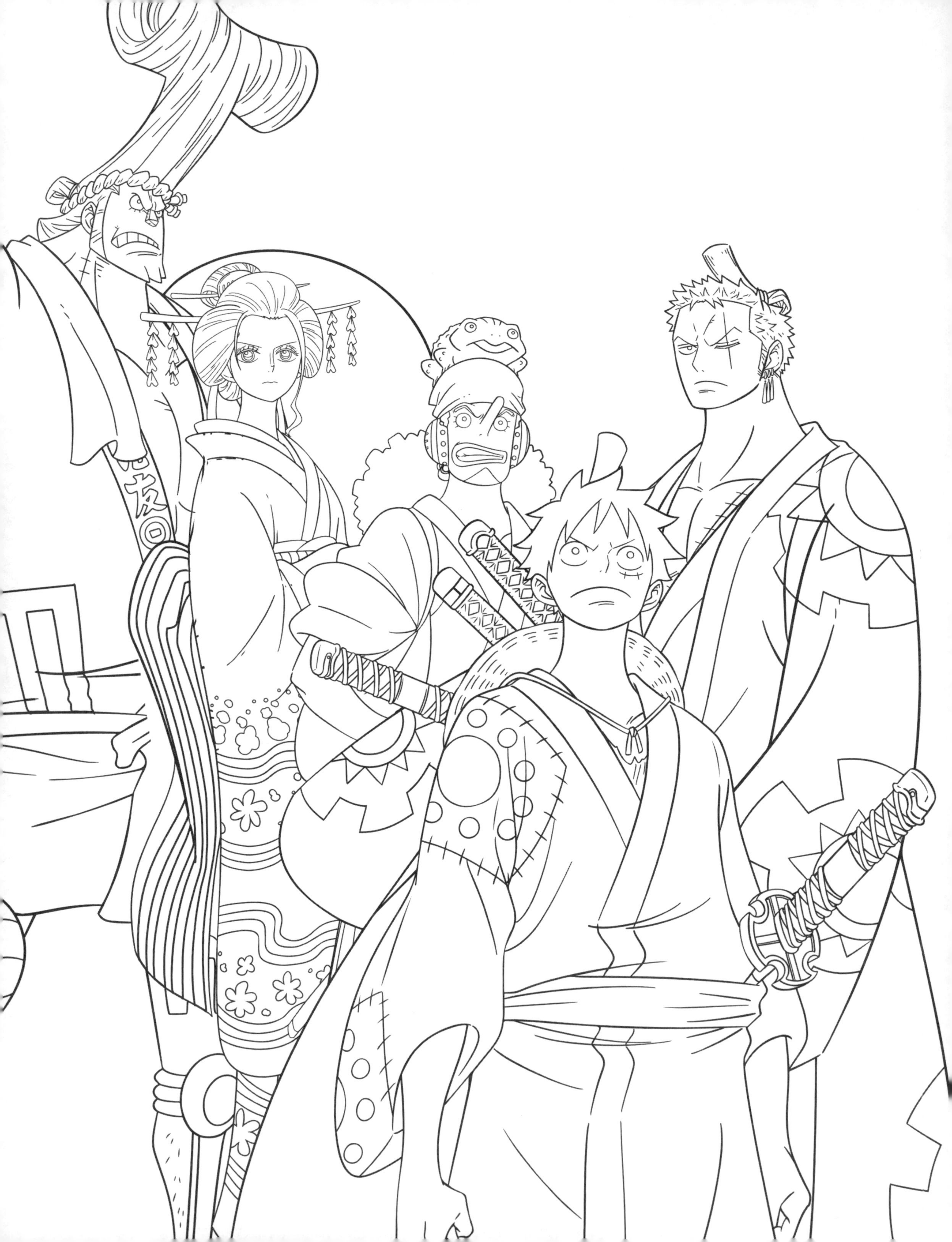

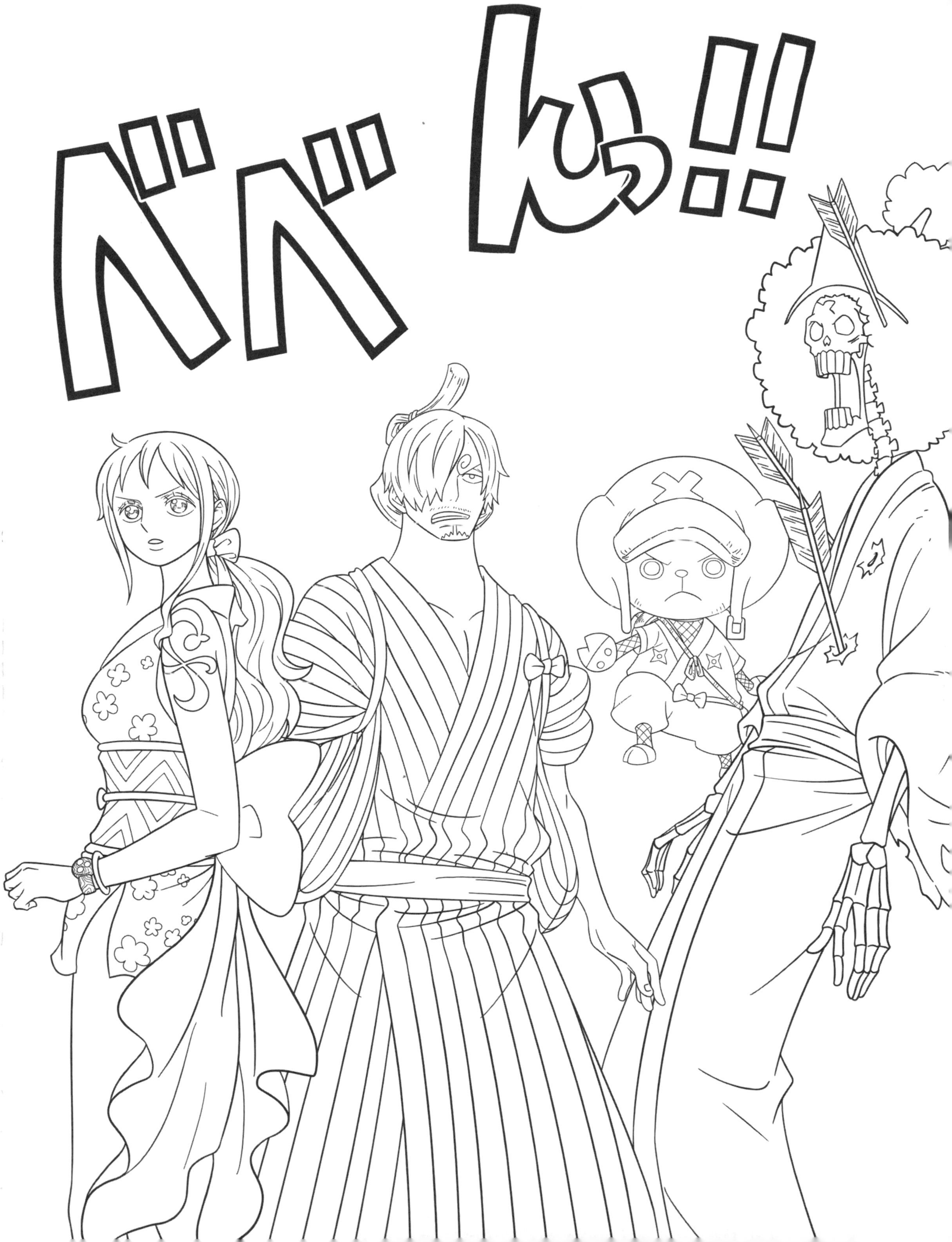

ババん!!

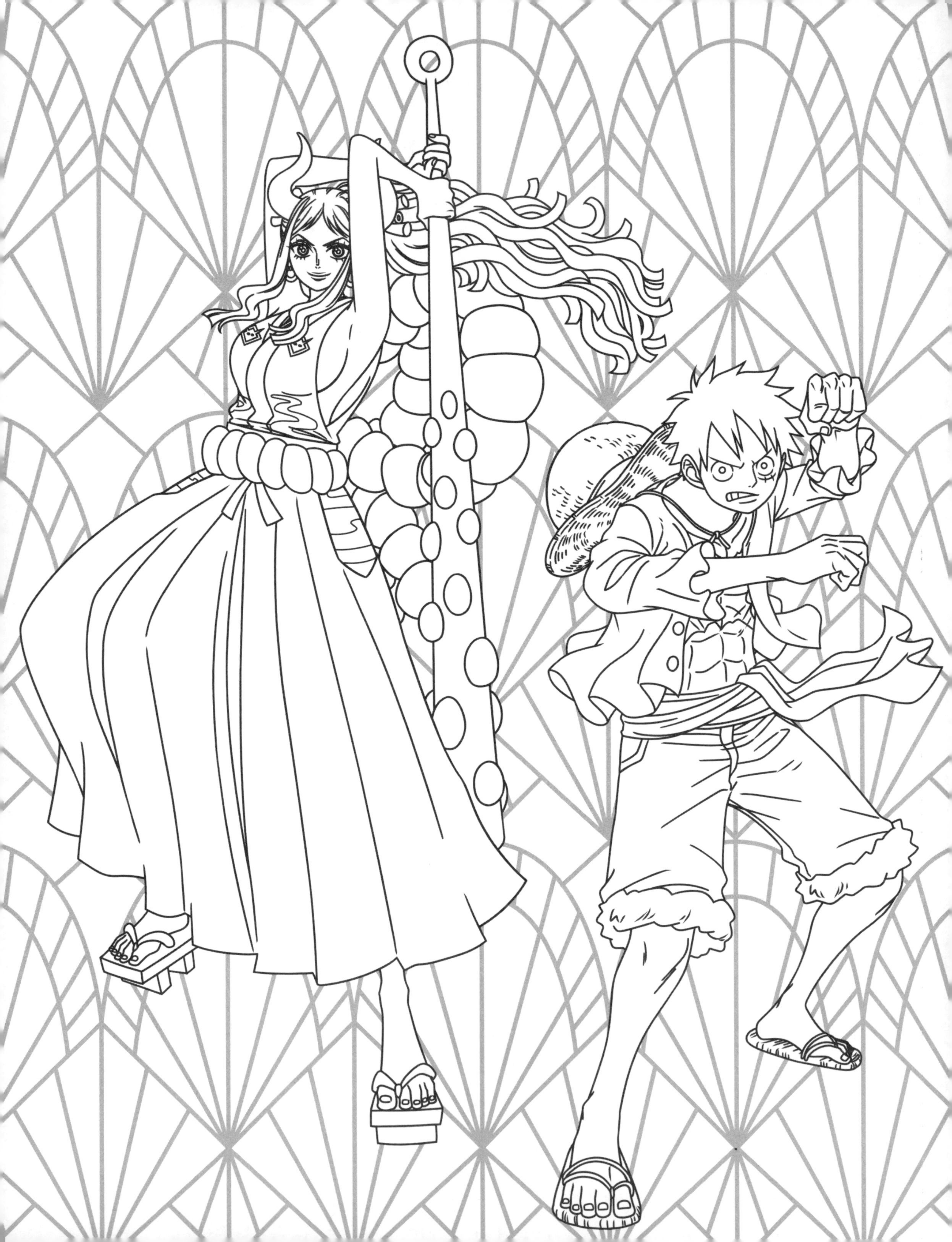

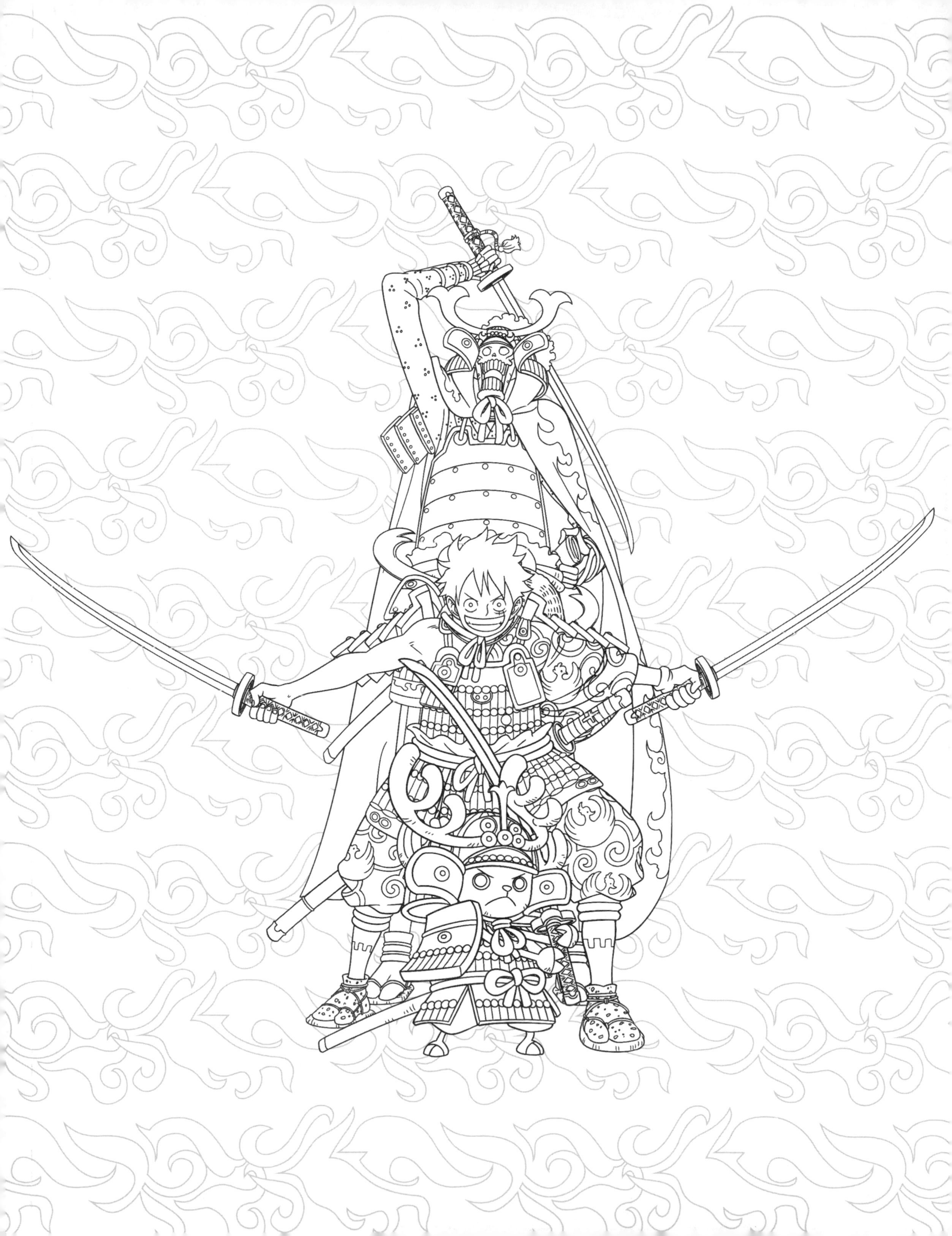

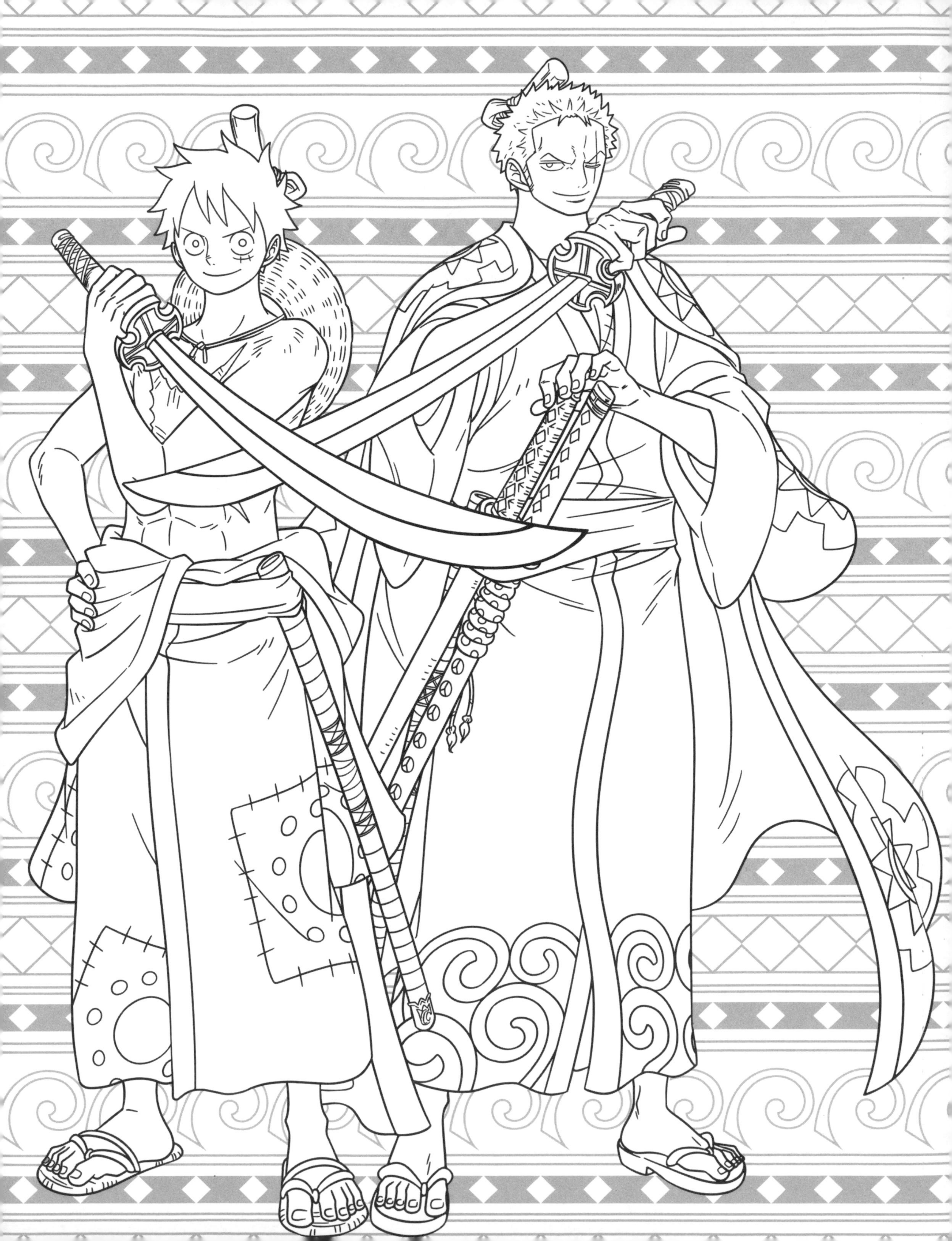

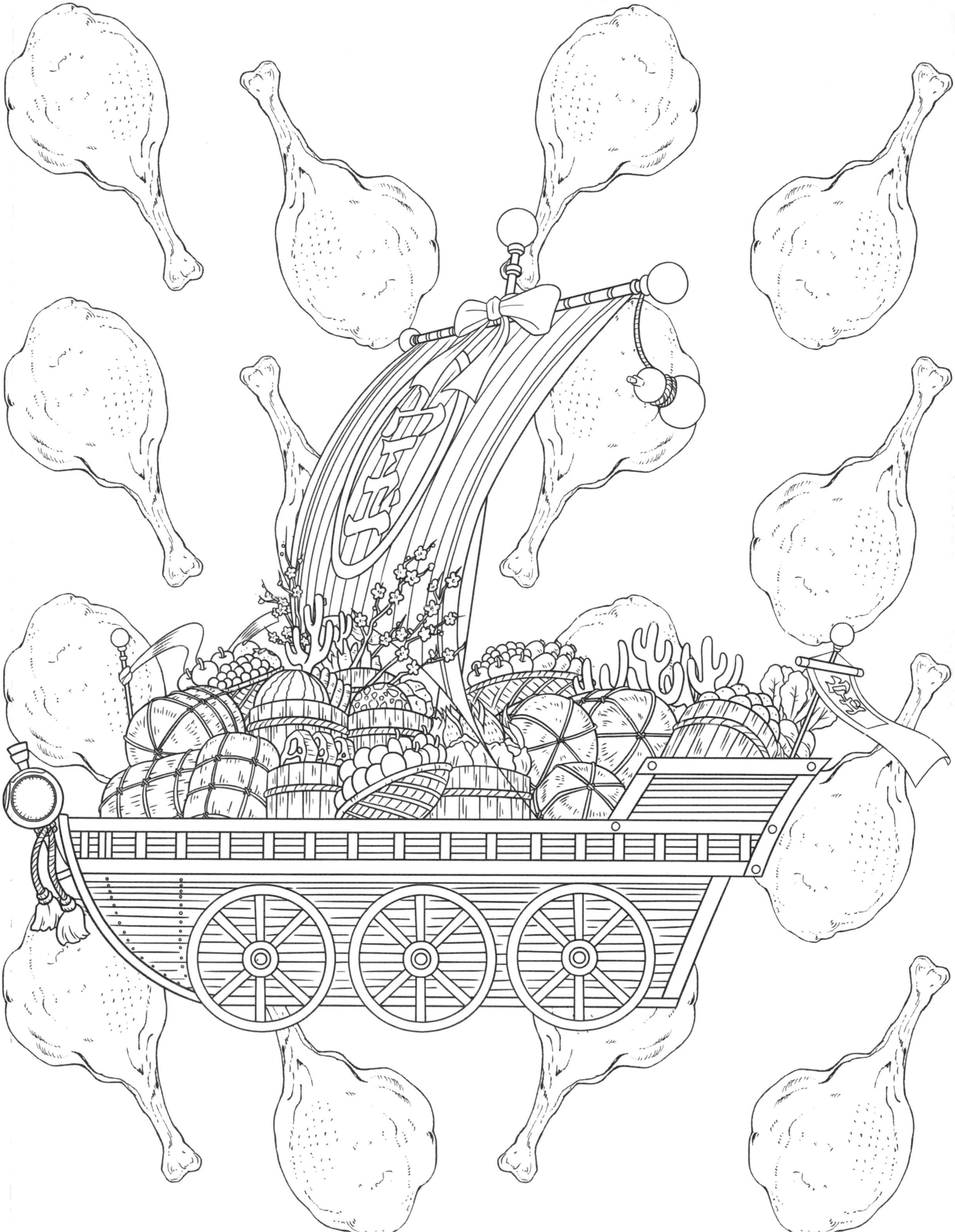

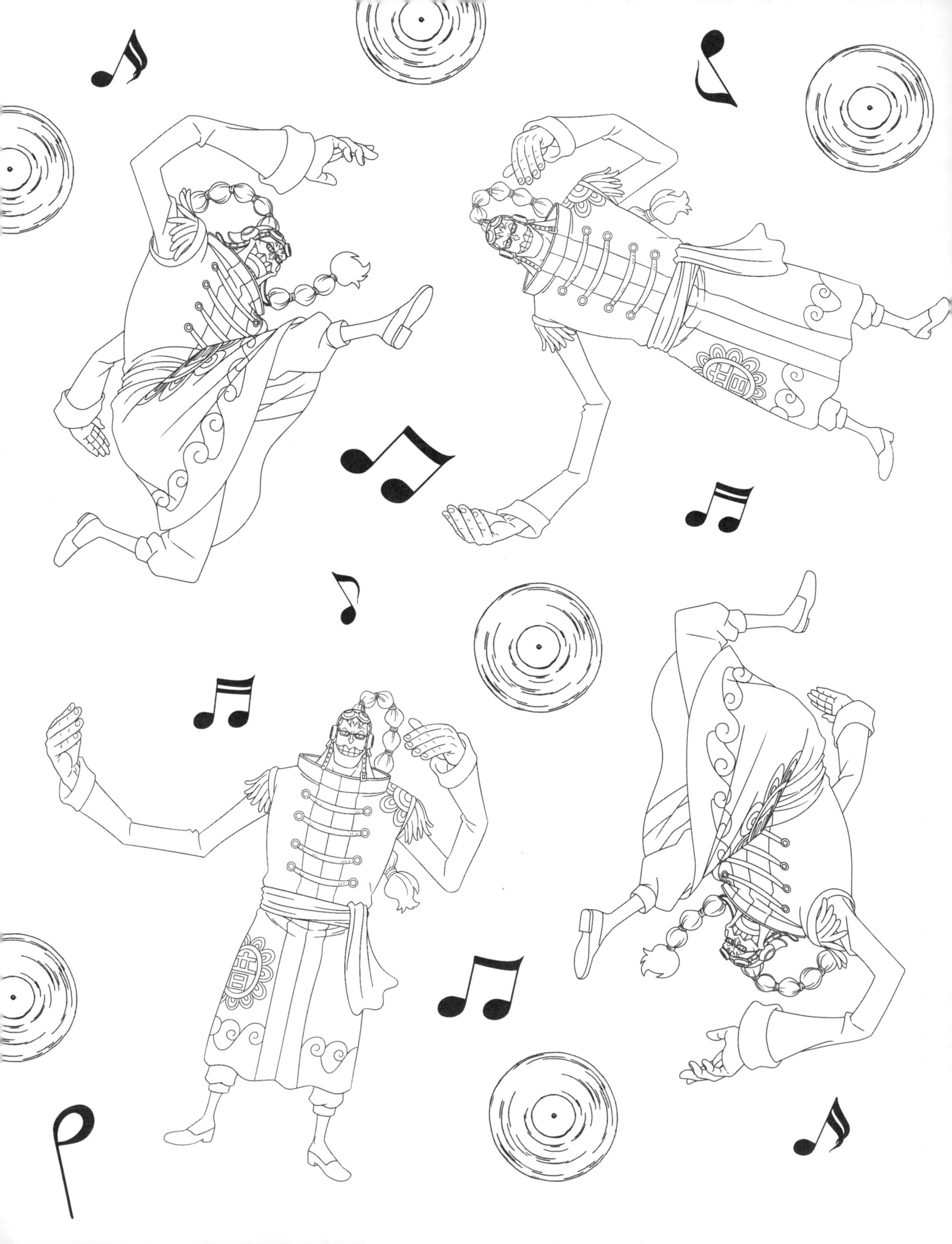

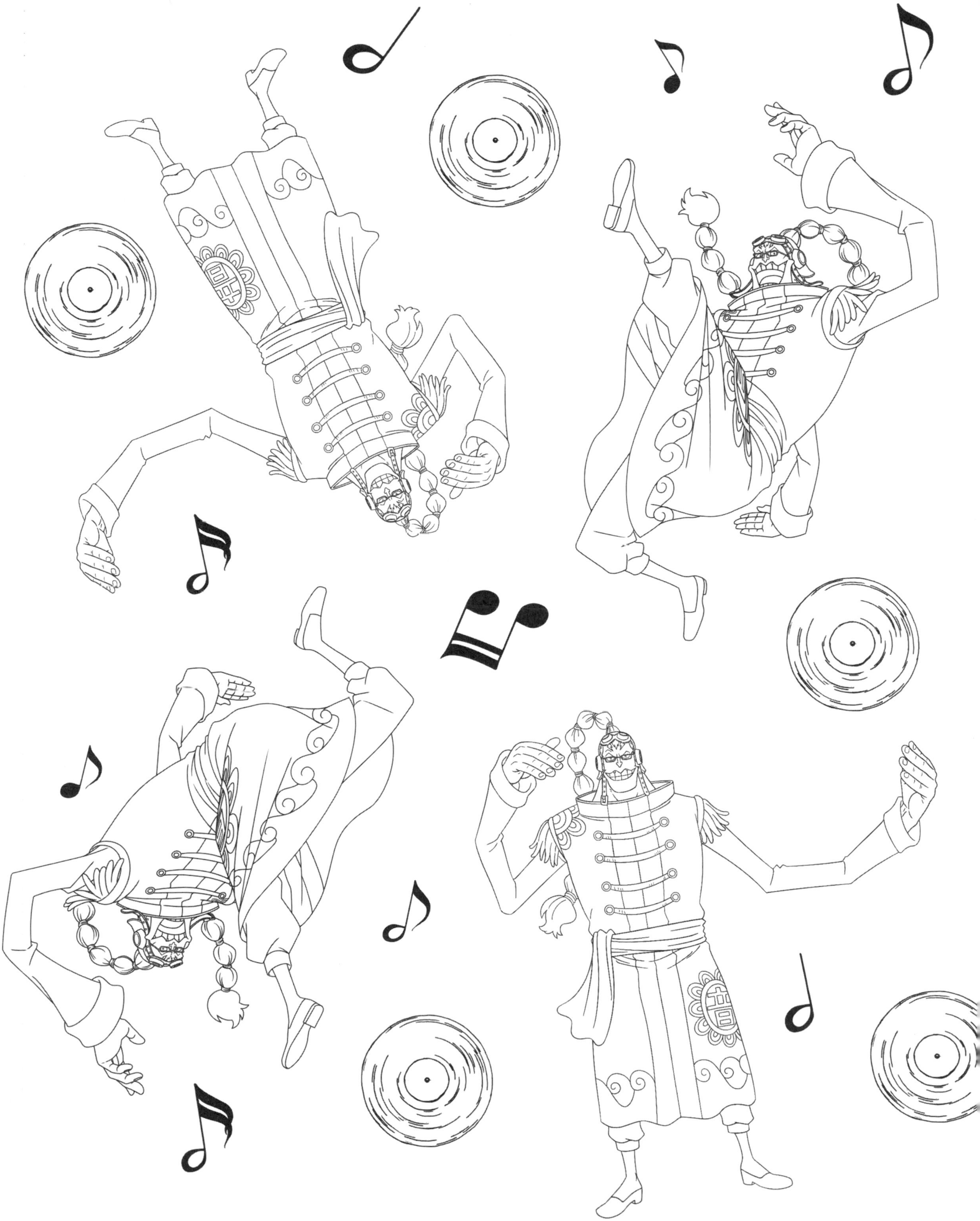

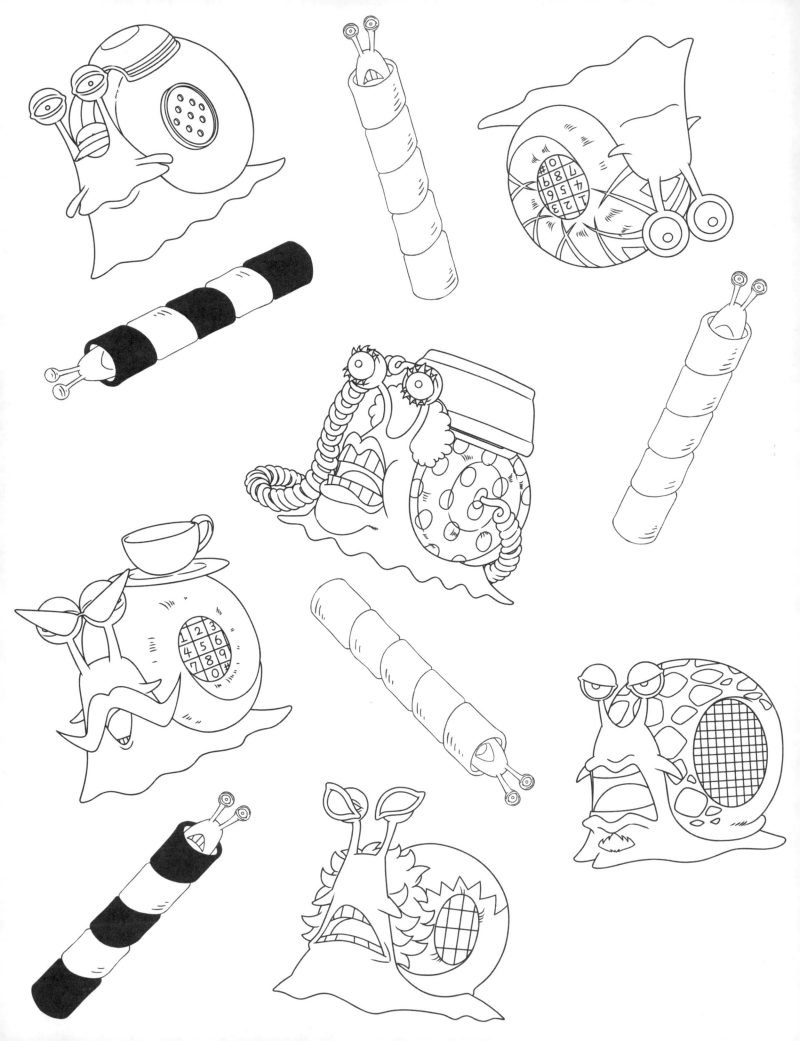

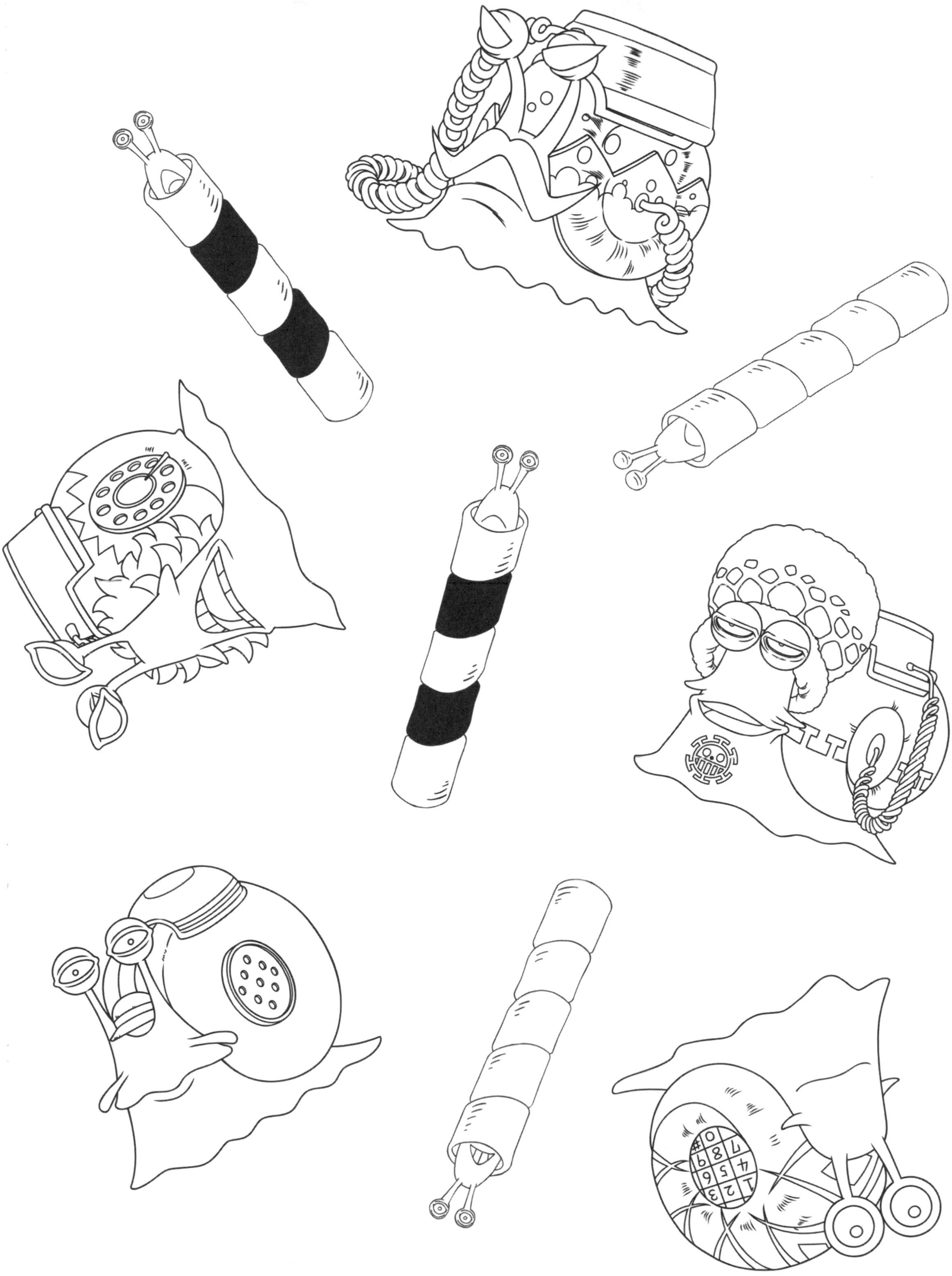

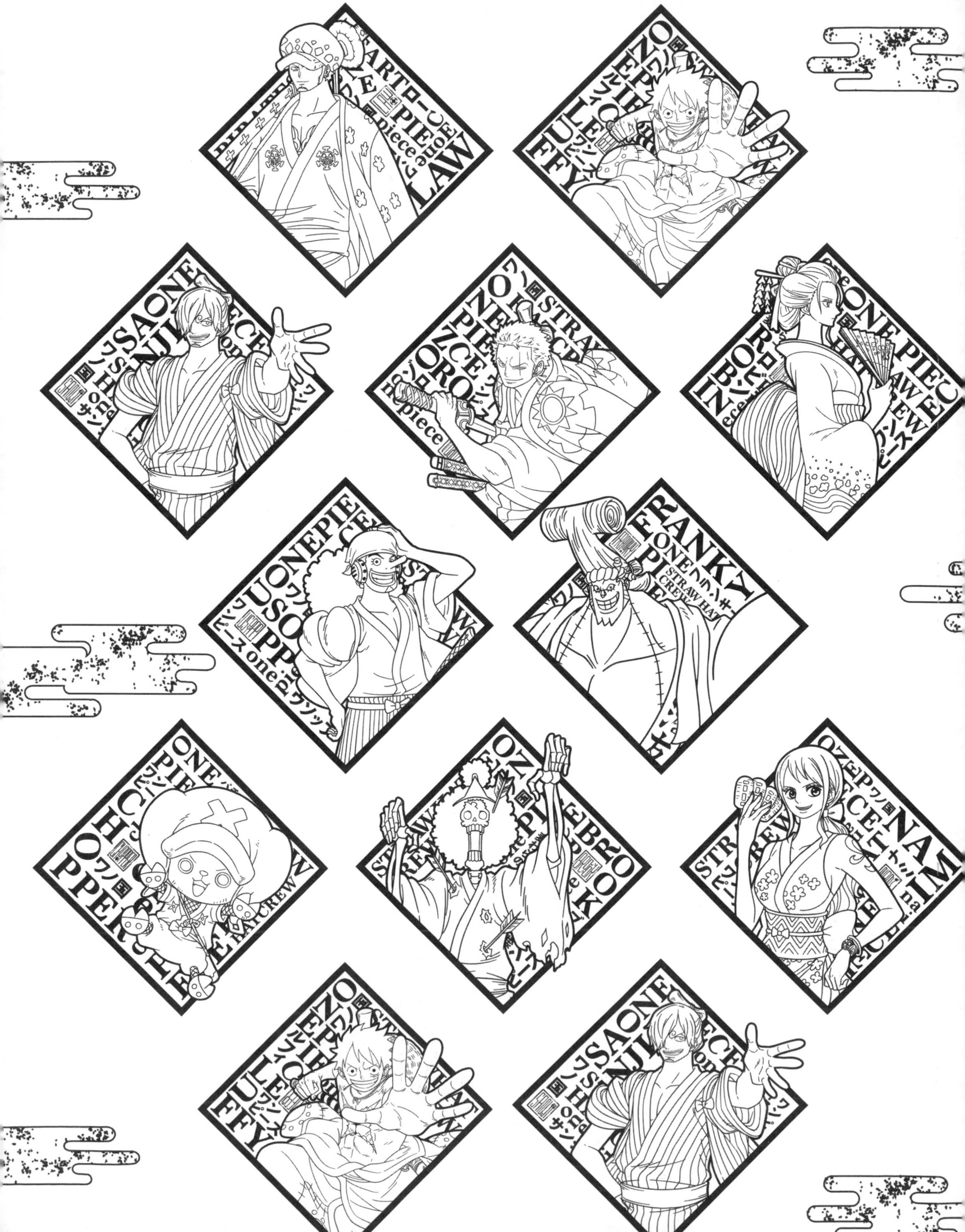
LAW
FRANKY
STRAW HAT CREW